They were wrapped in each other's arms and the mouth Abby had wanted from the night they had met was on hers, crushing hers.

It was consuming, blatant and fierce, and unthinking, her mouth opened in delicious reflex. Matteo's tongue went straight in, and yet she, too, sought his, like some exotic sword fight where both were winners as they partook in the deepest, sexiest kiss.

God, he was shameless, Abby thought. Then he took the energy of their kiss and didn't just sustain it; Matteo heightened it. He was hard and pressing into her and she could feel every delicious inch. His hands were now traveling down to her bottom and pulling her into him. Yet, rather than pull back, Abby was just as on fire as he.

And then they remembered the rules and pulled their mouths rather than their bodies back.

"When we win...we kiss," Matteo said.

She could live with that.

They were breathing so hard just staring at each other.

"When we place, we kiss," he said, kissing her cheek as if it were her mouth, and that made her laugh. "And if we lose," he continued, making out with her ear, "then we have to commiserate..."

The Billionaire's Legacy

A search for truth and the promise of passion!

For nearly sixty years, Italian billionaire Giovanni Di Sione has kept a shocking secret. Now, nearing the end of his days, he wants his grandchildren to know their true heritage.

He sends them each on a journey to find his "Lost Mistresses," a collection of love tokens— the only remaining evidence of his lost identity, his lost history...his lost love.

With each item collected, the Di Sione siblings take one step closer to the truth... and embark on a passionate journey that none could have expected!

Find out what happens in

The Billionaire's Legacy

Di Sione's Innocent Conquest by Carol Marinelli

The Di Sione Secret Baby by Maya Blake

To Blackmail a Di Sione by Rachel Thomas

The Return of the Di Sione Wife by Caitlin Crews

Di Sione's Virgin Mistress by Sharon Kendrick

A Di Sione for the Greek's Pleasure by Kate Hewitt

A Deal for the Di Sione Ring by Jennifer Hayward

The Last Di Sione Claims His Prize by Maisey Yates

Collect all 8 volumes!

Carol Marinelli

DI SIONE'S INNOCENT CONQUEST

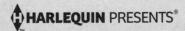

Recycling programs
for this product may
not exist in your area.

ISBN-13: 978-0-373-13447-2

Di Sione's Innocent Conquest

First North American Publication 2016

Copyright © 2016 by Harlequin Books S.A.

Special thanks and acknowledgment are given to Carol Marinelli for her contribution to The Billionaire's Legacy series.

HARLEQUIN®
www.Harlequin.com

Printed in U.S.A.

Carol Marinelli is a Taurus, with Taurus rising, yet still thinks she is a secret Gemini. Originally from England, she now lives in Australia and is the single mother of three. Apart from her children, writing romance and the friendships forged along the way are her passion. She chooses to believe in a happy-ever-after for all and strives for that in her writing.

Books by Carol Marinelli

Harlequin Presents

The Playboy of Puerto Banús
Playing the Dutiful Wife
Heart of the Desert
The Only Woman to Defy Him
More Precious than a Crown
Protecting the Desert Princess

Irresistible Russian Tycoons

The Price of His Redemption
The Cost of the Forbidden
Billionaire Without a Past
Return of the Untamed Billionaire

Playboys of Sicily

Sicilian's Shock Proposal
His Sicilian Cinderella

The Chatsfield

Princess's Secret Baby

Empire of the Sands

Banished to the Harem
Beholden to the Throne

Visit the Author Profile page at Harlequin.com for more titles.

PROLOGUE

MATTEO DI SIONE knew only too well his shortcomings.

He didn't need to have them pointed out to him.

Again.

Summoned by his grandfather, Giovanni, it was with a sense of dread that Matteo drove towards the Di Sione estate—a magnificent, sprawling residence set in the Gold Coast of Long Island.

On the death of Matteo's parents, Giovanni had taken in the seven orphans that his son, Benito, and wife, Anna, had left behind. For Matteo, then only five years old, this place had become home.

Now he had a penthouse apartment in Manhattan with glittering views of the skyline and the city that never slept at his feet.

This was home though.

For better or worse, this was where his fractured, scattered family met on occasion, or returned to at times.

Now, Matteo assumed that he had been called here to be served a lecture.

Another one.

The previous weekend had been particularly wild, even by Matteo's licentious standards. The press, who were eagerly awaiting his downfall, had been watching. They couldn't wait for a Di Sione to hit skid row and so had taken delight in reporting Matteo's million-dollar loss in Vegas on Saturday night. They had, of course, failed to mention that he had recouped the loss twice over by dawn. What hurt him the most, though, was that a prestigious paper had written a very scathing piece.

Arriving in Manhattan this morning, he had gone from his jet to the waiting car and checked the news—the headline he had seen had been the one he had dreaded the most.

History Repeats!

There was a photo of him coming out of the casino, unshaven, with his hair falling over his eyes. He was clearly a little the worse for wear. On his arm was a blonde.

Beside that image, there was another, taken some thirty years ago, in the very same year that he had been born.

Benito Di Sione coming out of a casino, unshaven with the same straight black hair falling over the same navy eyes and clearly a little the worse for wear. On his arm the beautiful requisite blonde, who was not Matteo's mother.

Matteo doubted his father would have remembered who the woman was, whereas Matteo always remembered his lovers.

On Saturday night her name had been Lacey and she had been gorgeous.

He adored women.

Skinny ones, big ones and anywhere in between. Matteo had a slight yen for the newly divorced—he had found that they were only too happy to rekindle that long-lost flame of desire.

Matteo always made it perfectly clear that he was here for a good time not a long time and he was never with anyone long enough to cheat.

The article had gone on to list the similarities between father and youngest son—the risk-taking, the decadent, debauched lifestyle—and had warned that Matteo was heading towards the same fate that had befallen his father—dead, his car wrapped around a lamppost and his wife deceased by his side.

No, Matteo was not looking forward to speaking with his grandfather; after all, Giovanni often said the very same thing.

He drove into the huge estate and looked ahead rather than taking in the luxurious surrounds, for they held few happy memories.

Still, it was home and, as he parked his car and walked towards the mansion where the Di Sione children had been raised, he wondered as to his reception. Matteo stopped by fairly regularly and took Giovanni out to his club for lunch whenever he could.

He knocked on the door simply to be polite but, as he did, he let himself in with his own key.

'It's Matteo,' he called out as he opened the door and then smiled when he saw Alma, the housekeeper, up on a stepladder.

'Master Matteo!' Alma mustn't have heard him knock because she jumped a little. She was working on a large flower display in the entrance hall and went to get down from the ladder but he gestured for her to carry on.

'Where is he?' Matteo asked.

'In his study. Do you want me to let Signor Giovanni know that you are here?'

'No, I'll just go straight through.' Matteo rolled his eyes. 'I believe he's expecting me.'

Alma gave him a small smile and Matteo took it to be a sympathetic one. Of course she must have seen the newspaper when she had taken Giovanni his breakfast this morning.

'How is he doing?' Matteo asked as he often did.

'He wants to speak with you himself,' Alma said and Matteo frowned at the vague answer.

He walked down a long hallway and then stood at the heavy mahogany door of his grandfather's study and took a steadying breath, then knocked on the door. When his grandfather's voice called for him to come in, he did so.

'Hey!' Matteo said as he opened the door.

He looked not to his grandfather but to the folded newspaper that lay on Giovanni's desk and, even as he closed the door behind him, Matteo set the tone. 'I've already seen it and I really don't need a lecture.'

'Where does lecturing you get me, Matteo?' Giovanni responded.

Matteo looked up at the sound of his grandfather's tired voice, and what he saw made his heart sink in dread. Giovanni looked not just pale, but so incredibly frail. His hair was as white as snow and his usually bright blue eyes seemed faded, and suddenly Matteo changed his mind—he wanted a lecture now! He wanted his grandfather to have brought him here to haul him over the proverbial coals, to tell Matteo that he must grow up, settle down and cease his hedonistic days. Anything other than what, Matteo had the terrible feeling, was about to come.

'I've asked you to come here to tell you...' Giovanni started but Matteo did not want to hear it. A master in diversion, he picked up the newspaper from his grandfather's desk and unfolded it.

'For all their comparisons they forget one vital piece of information,' Matteo said. '*He* had responsibilities.'

'I know that he did,' Giovanni said, 'but you have responsibility too. To yourself. Matteo, you are heading for trouble. The company you keep, the risks you take...'

'Are mine to take,' Matteo interrupted. 'My father was married and had seven children when he died.' He jabbed at the photo. 'Well, seven that he had admitted to!'

'Matteo!' Giovanni said. This was not going as he intended. 'Sit down.'

'No!' He argued not with his grandfather but himself. 'For all they compare me to him they deliberately omit to mention that I don't have a wife and children. I'd never put anyone through the hell he made.'

He never would.

It was a decision Matteo had made a long time ago.

He was single and staying that way.

Giovanni looked at his grandson and he worried for him.

Fun-loving and charismatic, Matteo not only acted like his father at times, he looked like him too. They had the same navy eyes, the same straight nose and even their hair fell forwards in the same way.

Giovanni, for his own private reasons, had never bonded with his son. He had never told anyone why; it was a secret he had intended to take to his grave.

In the aftermath of Benito's and Anna's deaths, five-year-old Matteo, a carbon copy of his father, had been too much of a visual reminder of Benito for Giovanni and, rather than learning from his mistakes, he had repeated them, and Giovanni had kept his distance from his grandson.

Matteo had run wild and that irrepressible personality had gone largely unchecked. When he had dropped out of college after just a year, a terrible row had ensued. Matteo had said that he didn't need to be taught about the business world—playing the stock market was in his DNA and he wanted to set up a hedge fund rather than sit in lectures—and Giovanni had told his grandson that he was just like his father and that he feared he was heading the same way. Accusations that Matteo had not needed to hear and certainly not from his grandfather.

It was too late to tame him. Giovanni had shouted at the young man, and Matteo had fought back.

'You never once tried!' It was the only glimpse Matteo had ever given to another of the pain he carried. 'You never once fought for me,' he had shouted. 'You left me to roam this house and make my own way. Don't act now as if you care.' Yes, harsh words had been said and their relationship still bore the scars to this day.

'Take a seat, Matteo,' Giovanni said.

Matteo didn't do as asked.

Troubled by his grandfather's appearance and unsettled as to what was to come, instead of sitting down, he walked over to the window. He looked out to the vast estate that had once been his playground.

Matteo's grandmother had died before he had been born, so his younger sisters had been taken care of by his older sister, Allegra, while his older siblings had all headed off to boarding school.

Matteo had pretty much been left to his own devices.

'Do you remember when you used to visit me as children when your parents were still alive?' Giovanni asked.

'I don't think about that time,' Matteo answered.

He did his best to never look back.

'You were very young, of course. Maybe you can't remember...'

Oh, Matteo did.

He remembered only too well life before the Di Sione children had come to live here. He could still recall, with painful clarity, the fights that could erupt at any given time and just the sheer chaos of their existence. Of course, he hadn't understood then that there were drugs involved. Matteo had just known that his family lived on the edge.

A luxurious knife edge.

'Matteo.' Giovanni broke into his dark thoughts. 'Do you remember when I used to tell you all the story of the Lost Mistresses?'

'No.' Matteo shrugged and dismissed the conversation. As he looked out of the window to the lake, his gaze fell on a tree that was so high his stomach churned as he remembered climbing it and falling.

A branch had broken his fall. Had it not, he'd probably have died.

No one had seen and no one had known.

Alma, the housekeeper, had scolded him for the grass stains on his clothes and had asked what had happened.

'I tripped near the lake,' he had said.

His ribs and head had hurt and his heart had still been pounding, not that he would let Alma see that.

Instead it had been easier to lie.

The sensation of falling still woke Matteo to this day but that wasn't all that he recalled as he stood there staring out of the window. There was a darker memory that he had never shared, one that could still bring him out in a cold sweat—pleading with his father to stop, to slow down, to please take him home.

From that day to this, Matteo had never again revealed fear.

It got you nowhere. If anything, it spurred others on.

'You surely remember,' Giovanni insisted. 'The Lost Mistresses…'

'I don't.' He shook his head.

'Then I'll remind you.'

As if I need to hear this again, Matteo thought! He said nothing, though, and let the old man speak.

'Don't ask me how I came by them, for an old man must have his secrets…' Giovanni started. Matteo remained standing, his face impassive, as his grandfather recited the tale. 'But when I came to America, I had in my possession trinkets, my Lost Mistresses. They meant more to me than you can ever know but in order to survive I was forced to sell them. My Lost Mistresses, the love of my life, we owe them everything.' Giovanni stopped speaking for a moment and looked at Matteo's pale features and unshaven jaw, which was now clenched. 'You do remember.'

'No.' Matteo was getting annoyed now. 'I've told you I don't.' He loathed delving into the past and he didn't want a trip down memory lane today. 'Do you want to go out?' he suggested. 'I could take you for a drive. We could go to your club…'

'Matteo.' Giovanni cut him off. He knew that Matteo was trying to change the subject. He loved his grandson very much. Even if they had had their problems, still Matteo came by often and took him out. He just, Giovanni knew, let no one in.

Giovanni had to put things right while he still could. 'I have to tell you something.'

'Come on, we'll go for a drive…' Matteo pushed. He did not want to be here and he did not want to hear what he knew his grandfather was about to tell him.

'I'm dying, Matteo.'

Giovanni watched his grandson for his reaction but Matteo never gave his true feelings away.

'We're all dying,' Matteo responded, trying to make light of the devastating news while his heart pounded in his chest, as still his mind fought to deny the truth.

He did not want to have this conversation.

He could not stand to think of his grandfather gone and his family together at another funeral. Images of his parents' coffins and the children all walking behind them still appeared in magazines at times and were always in his mind.

He did not want his grandfather to die.

'The leukemia is back,' Giovanni said.

'What about that treatment you had?' Matteo asked. Seventeen years ago they had nearly lost Giovanni. A bone marrow donor had been needed and all the grandchildren had been tested but none of them had returned a match. It had been then that the eldest, Alessandro, had confessed that he knew their father had another son. They had tracked Nate down and he had returned a match. 'Couldn't Nate...'

'A transplant is out of the question, and I'm not sure that treatment is the best way forward at this stage,' Giovanni said. 'The doctors say we can hope for remission but, failing that, it is a matter of months. The reality is, I have a year at best.'

'You know how I loathe reality,' Matteo said and the old man smiled.

'I do.'

And Matteo escaped reality often—in casinos, clubs, daredevil escapades, constantly pushing both his body and the hedge fund he had set up to the very brink.

How Giovanni wished he could take back the damaging words he had said and handled this complex man so much better. Yes, while there were many similarities between Matteo and his father, there were other traits too—there was an innate kindness to Matteo that had been absent in Benito, a rare kindness of which Giovanni was immensely proud. And though Matteo was eternally restless, in other ways he was the most patient man Giovanni had ever known. As his health had deteriorated, as his stamina had waned, it was Matteo who would come around and take him out, Matteo who fell easily into a slower step beside him and let Giovanni ramble as he had just done.

'Matteo, I want you to do something for me. I have something that I need for you to do if I am going to go to my grave content.'

Matteo took a breath and braced himself for the inevitable. Here came the lecture! He was quite sure he was about to be told to settle down and tame his ways and so he frowned when the old man voiced his thoughts.

'I want you to bring me one of my Lost Mistresses.'

Matteo turned and looked at his grandfather and wondered if he'd finally lost his mind. 'What on earth are you talking about?'

'My Lost Mistresses!' Giovanni went into one of the drawers in his desk and Matteo saw a flare of excitement in the old man's eyes as he took out a photo. Giovanni's hand was shaking as he handed it to Matteo.

'This necklace is one of my Lost Mistresses.'

Matteo looked at the photo. It was a lavish emerald necklace and it was, quite simply, beautiful. 'White gold?' he checked and Giovanni shook his head.

'Platinum.'

The emeralds were amazing—the size of robins' eggs, they sparkled and beguiled. They were so beautiful that even their image made Matteo reach out to run his finger over the stones. 'We thought it was just a tale that you told, that they were some old coins or something.'

'So you *do* remember!'

Matteo conceded that he did with a half smile. 'Yes, I remember you telling us your tale.' He let out a low whistle as he looked at the necklace again. 'This would be worth…' Usually he could pick this sort of thing but in this instance he really didn't know. 'Millions?' he loosely gauged.

'And some.'

'Who's the designer?' he asked. 'What jewellery house…?'

'Unknown,' Giovanni quickly said and Matteo frowned because surely a piece of jewellery as exquisite as this would have some considerable history attached.

'Is this how you got your start?' he asked. He could see it a little more clearly. Di Sione had started as a shipping empire but now the name was global. If Giovanni had sold pieces as exquisite as this one, then Matteo could see how it might have transpired. Yet, how could a young man from Sicily come to be in possession of this?

Giovanni was less than forthcoming, though, when Matteo pushed for answers.

'I just want you to find it for me,' Giovanni said. 'I don't know where to start. I sold it to a man named Roche some sixty years ago. Since then it's been sold on.' Matteo could see that his grandfather was getting distressed and knew that this necklace really meant something to him.

'How did you come to own this?' he asked again.

'Don't ask me how I came by them, for an old man must have his secrets...' Giovanni said and Matteo gave another half smile.

Now the tale of old made a bit more sense.

'Matteo, I want that necklace. Whatever it takes. Can you find it and bring it to me?'

He looked over to his grandfather.

How he wished he could open up and tell the old man that he meant something to him, that he understood how hard the years had been on him. But Matteo was incapable of giving anyone more than a loan of that smile or body. His mind was a closed door.

So instead he nodded.

This he could do.

'You know that I shall.'

Giovanni got out of his chair and walked over to Matteo and wrapped his grandson in an embrace, something Giovanni wished he had done more of all those years ago.

Just for a moment, Matteo let himself be held, but then he pulled back.

'Come on, then,' he said, pocketing the picture in his jacket.

'Where?'

'Your club,' Matteo said and rattled his keys but then he changed his mind.

His grandfather was dying.

There was no way that he'd be driving today.

Giovanni called for his driver.

CHAPTER ONE

MATTEO DIDN'T LIKE HIM.

Not that it showed in his expression.

He just sat in Ellison's study and glanced up at the hunting trophies that lined the walls and then back to the man.

'Do I look like I need the money?' Ellison sneered.

Matteo shrugged, refusing to let the other man see that he was surprised by his response to a very generous offer.

He had been unable to find out the designer or jewellery house that the necklace had come from but had found out that Roche had sold it on to Hugo Ellison some twenty or so years ago.

Matteo vaguely knew Ellison from fundraising galas he had attended and he also knew that the man was money and power mad. He had been sure it would only take a generous donation to his political fund to secure the necklace and had set off for the meeting cocksure and confident that he would leave with what he wanted.

Now Matteo wasn't so sure.

'It was a gift to my late wife,' Ellison said.

Matteo knew enough about that marriage to be sure that Ellison wasn't crying himself to sleep at night over her death but he went along with the game. 'I'm sorry,' he said and then stood. 'It was insensitive of me to ask.' He held out his hand. 'Thank you for seeing me though.'

Ellison didn't offer his hand and when he didn't conclude the meeting, Matteo knew, even before Ellison spoke, that he held the ace—it was just a matter of time before the necklace was his.

'Actually,' Ellison said, 'it seems a shame to keep it locked up.' He looked at Matteo. 'Sit down, son.'

He loathed it when people said that.

It was just a power play, a chance to assert a stronger position, but Matteo knew he had the upper hand and so he went along with it and took a seat again.

I really *don't like you*, Matteo thought as Ellison poured them both a drink.

'How come you're interested in the necklace?' Ellison asked.

'I appreciate beauty,' he answered and Ellison gave a smug smile.

'And me.'

Ellison knew who Matteo was, of course. Everyone knew the Di Siones and he knew Matteo's reputation with women.

Yes, Matteo appreciated beauty.

'Didn't you date Princess…?'

'I don't date,' Matteo interrupted and Ellison laughed.

'Good call. So, how far are you prepared to go?'

'How much do you want?' Matteo asked.

'Not how much, how far?' Ellison corrected. 'I believe you like a challenge.'

'I do.'

'And from what I've read about you, impossible odds don't daunt you.'

'They don't.'

They thrilled Matteo, in fact.

'See this.' Ellison beckoned for him to stand and Matteo walked over and they stood staring at a portrait of Ellison and his late wife, Anette, and their two daughters. 'This was taken at our charity gala some twelve years ago.'

'Your wife was a very beautiful woman.' And very rich, Matteo thought. A lot of Ellison's wealth had come from her family and Matteo privately wondered just how far Ellison's political career would have gone without Anette's billions.

'Anette knew how to play the game,' Ellison said. 'We had a terrible fight the day before that photo was taken. She'd found out that I was sleeping with my assistant, but you wouldn't know it from that photo.'

'No.' Matteo looked at Anette's smiling face as she stood by her man. 'You wouldn't.'

Ellison's revelation didn't shock Matteo; instead it wearied him.

He peered at Ellison's daughters. They were both immaculate—one was dressed in oyster grey, the other in beige, and both were wearing the requisite pearls. One had her hair neatly up and the other... A small smile played on Matteo's lips as he examined the younger daughter more closely. Her dark wavy hair, despite a velvet band, was untamed and her eyes were angry. Her smile was forced and it looked as if the hand her father had on her shoulder was not a proud display of affection, more that it was there to hold her down.

'That's Abby.'

Ellison's sigh as he said her name told Matteo that Abby was the bane of his existence.

'Look at this one,' Ellison said and they moved on to the next photo. 'It must have been...' Ellison thought back. 'I think Abby's about five here, so some twenty-two years ago.'

Abby's eyes were red, Matteo noted.

Well, they were actually a vivid green but she'd clearly been crying.

'The only way we could get her to sit in a dress for the photo was to give her a toy car. She was obsessed with cars even then.'

Matteo had no idea where this was leading but he had learned long ago that all knowledge was power and so he let Ellison drone on. He could also see that in the photo Anette was wearing the necklace that Giovanni so badly wanted.

'Abby was upset because we'd just fired the nanny. Both the girls were terribly fond of her,' Ellison said. 'My wife insisted on it though.'

Now they were getting somewhere! Matteo guessed that it wasn't just the daughters who'd been fond of the nanny.

'And this,' Ellison said, moving along, 'is the last photo I have of my daughter in a dress.'

There Abby stood on a red carpet, with a good-looking blond man by her side.

A man Matteo thought that he recognised.

'Hunter Coleman ,' Ellison said and Matteo nodded as he now placed him. Hunter was a top racing driver and had a reputation with women that rivalled even Matteo's. 'Abby dated him for a while,' Ellison explained. 'Anyway, as I said, she always had a thing for cars. If I couldn't find her, then she'd be in the garage, pulling apart a Bentley, or taking the engine out of a Jag. I tried to get her out of it—it's not exactly fitting for a young woman of her standing. She went off to college to study fashion and started dating Hunter and finally I thought that the tomboy in her was gone. The trouble is, unlike her mother, my darling daughter doesn't know how to stand and offer quiet support. No, Abby, being Abby, had to offer a top racing driver advice on his racing technique.'

Matteo laughed but then it trailed off.

Hunter's hand was closed tightly around Abby's, and again, despite the smile, her eyes were…not angry. Matteo looked more closely.

Guarded.

It was the best he could come up with—but no, despite the smile for the camera, that wasn't a happy young woman.

'Anyway, she dumped him!' Ellison sounded shocked. 'God knows how she thought she could do better, and then she switched from studying fashion to automotive engineering. Now she's…'

'The Boucher team!' Matteo could place her as well now. Well, not Abby specifically, but yes, he knew a little about the emerging racing team.

'Boucher was my wife's maiden name.' Ellison sighed. 'It's a very expensive hobby…'

'I can imagine.'

'Oh, believe me, you can't.' Ellison shook his head. 'Especially when the owner of the team refuses to play the corporate game and chat up sponsors. As I said to Abby last week, she's going to have to find the cash. I'm not bailing her out.'

'Has she asked?'

'Not yet!' Ellison's smug smile returned. 'But the rest of her mother's trust fund is tied up till she's thirty or married. There's no chance of *that* girl marrying, which means she's got no income for another three years!'

'Why are you telling me this?' Matteo asked.

'Because, as you must have heard, I'm on the comeback trail. In July I'm going to be holding my first political fundraiser since my wife's death. I've told Abby that if she comes, and looks the part, and by that I mean she loses the jeans and oil rags, then I'll give her a cash injection to tide her over.'

'Has she said that she's coming?'

'Not yet,' Ellison said. 'But I need her to be there. Image is everything in politics and I don't want there to be even a whiff of discord. Annabel, my eldest daughter, will do the right thing but I want Abby to be here too. I want my daughter, at my function, wearing her mother's necklace. I want her looking like a woman for once...'

She looked all woman to Matteo.

'Can you manage that?' Ellison asked.

'Sorry?' Matteo frowned.

'You said that you like a challenge. You like women—see if you can sweet-talk her and get Abby to show up here, looking the part. If she does, at the end of the night, the necklace is yours.'

'How am I supposed to persuade her if you can't...?' Matteo started but then, guessing Ellison's intent, he shook his head. 'No way.'

Ellison just laughed. 'I'm not asking you to seduce her. I don't think you'd get very far. Rumour has it my daughter isn't particularly interested in men.'

No, Matteo really, *really* didn't like this man.

'She hasn't dated anyone since Hunter and it

hasn't gone unnoticed,' Ellison said, frowning at the photo. 'I want that rumour quashed. I want Abby here, dressed like a woman and with a handsome chap by her side.' Ellison returned his gaze to Matteo and continued. 'You could be a potential sponsor, considering investing in her team.'

'It's April,' Matteo pointed out. 'Your fundraiser isn't until July. How long am I supposed to be *considering* investing for?'

'I'd be giving you the necklace for nothing, perhaps the money you've earmarked for it could go towards convincing my daughter that you want to sponsor the team.'

'And if she doesn't come to your fundraiser?'

'You don't get your necklace.'

Matteo could cheerfully have knocked Ellison's lights out but instead he watched as Ellison went over to the safe and took out a gleaming polished wooden box and handed it to him.

Oh, my God, Matteo thought as he undid the intricate latch and saw the necklace firsthand.

Not even the photos did it justice.

How the hell had his grandfather come by this? Matteo wondered, and he could see now why he would want it back.

Jewellery had never really impressed Matteo.

This piece couldn't fail to.

'I doubt it's possible to get Abby here,' Ellison said.

Matteo looked over to Ellison and then back to

the necklace and he took Ellison's words as a dare—
which was something he never said no to.

And his grandfather wanted the necklace so badly.

No, he could never be the man his grandfather
wanted him to be but this he could do.

'Can you give me your daughter's contact details?'
Matteo asked.

His mind was made up—he would get this Lost
Mistress back to where it belonged.

CHAPTER TWO

ELLISON HAD BEEN right about one thing—his daughter Abby really was terrible at the corporate stuff.

It had taken two weeks for her to reply to Matteo's email and at best her response had been lukewarm.

Of course Matteo had looked into the Boucher team more closely by then.

He was a risk-taker by nature, but they were, even by his standards, more of a gamble than one should take.

It was their second year in competition and their best was a fifth place last year. Frequently, they placed last or second last. Now they were competitors in the Henley Cup—a prestigious international event, held over three races.

They weren't considered a mention.

Matteo finally decided to call Abby but *effusive* wasn't a word that had sprung to mind when she told him that no, they couldn't meet, given that she was on her way to Dubai.

'So am I,' he, on impulse, had replied.

'Excuse me?'

'I've got a couple of racehorses that I want to look at and my sister Allegra is holding a charity event in May... Hold on.' Matteo checked his calendar. 'Yes, that's on Saturday the seventh. How about lunch on the Friday?'

'I won't be able to get away for lunch.'

'Dinner, then?' Matteo persisted and she returned his offer with a long stretch of silence. 'Breakfast?'

'Just stop by the track.'

'Sure,' he said. 'I'll look forward...'

She had already rung off.

The heat was fierce in Dubai.

And as for the humidity!

Suffice to say, with the hangover Matteo had, he would far rather be in the airconditioned comfort of his hotel than in the goldfish bowl of a racetrack. The sun seemed to be coming at him from all angles as he made his way to the Boucher sheds.

Matteo had been in Dubai for three days and what an amazing three days they had been. The first had consisted of a wild welcome on board his friend Sheikh Kedah's yacht.

Kedah seemed hell-bent on returning the wild week Matteo had given him on a recent trip to New York City. The second day had been spent galloping at breakneck speed with his friend along a beach. Matteo had taken a tumble and dislocated his shoulder. The sheikh had called for his private physician to put it back. With Matteo's arm strapped and a little out of action they had hit the racetracks and placed a few bets on a camel race. The potential two years' jail time for illegal betting had only served to give Matteo an extra high!

It had been a giddy introduction to Dubai but now he had crashed back to earth—the smell of oil was nauseating and the sound from the track had his molars aching. He'd lost the sling that the physician had provided and so his shoulder was killing him.

And Abby Ellison was nowhere to be seen.

It was after four and he wondered if she might have finished for the day. A group of guys were watching as Pedro, the Boucher driver, put the car through its paces. He knew it was Pedro because Matteo recognised the deep green of the Boucher car.

Matteo had done some further research on the team, of course.

They had entered in the prestigious Henley Cup. A series of three races—Dubai, Milan and Monte Carlo. The final race took place in July a week before Ellison's fundraiser.

As newcomers the Boucher team wasn't being taken seriously, especially because the owner was a woman. Just a little rich girl playing with her daddy's money seemed to be the general consensus.

Pedro Sanchez, their driver, was someone who

was being watched seriously though, and there were a couple of other teams who had their eye on him.

The group of men all ignored him and that suited Matteo just fine. He just drank from a large bottle of cola and idly watched.

Or rather, at first, he idly watched.

Matteo had never really been in to cars and not just because his parents had died in a crash. His father had once taken a five-year-old Matteo for a joy-ride.

There was no joy in that memory!

Still, this was different—Pedro was really putting the car through its paces now, hugging the bend, belting it down the straight, and the roar of the motor was, as it flew past him, a bit of a turn-on.

'Whoa!' one of the guys shouted as the car lost traction, but then Pedro skilfully righted it and Matteo watched as the car again sped down the straight and then slowed down as it came towards them.

'Hey...'

Matteo turned as someone greeted him and blinked in vague surprise. 'Pedro...' Matteo shook his hand; he recognised the young man himself from his research. 'Sorry for the double take. I thought that I was watching you out there. I didn't realise there were two drivers.'

'No, no...' Pedro said. 'Soon you'll get to see me drive. That's Abby—she's just checking out some adjustments that she has made.'

Matteo looked back at the car and, sure enough, climbing out from it, dressed in tight leather, was *no* man, and the vague turn-on Matteo had felt before was rather less vague now.

He hadn't known that he was in to leather either!

The racing world was looking up, he decided as she took off her helmet and the fire guard and then shook her long dark hair out.

She was tall enough to wear her curves well, and if she only smiled he would return it with the best of his. And Matteo's smile could melt. But then he remembered he was not here to seduce and so he kept his business expression on.

'So,' Pedro said, 'I hear that you have a meeting with Abby.'

'I do.'

'Good,' Pedro responded and he could hear the slight edge to the man's voice. 'Then I guess it's time for me to show you a little of what I can do.' He looked over to Abby, who had reached them now. 'How is she?'

'Oh, she's running like silk now.'

They spoke as if the car was a person!

'I've warmed her up for you,' Abby said and then, as Pedro headed off towards the car, she finally acknowledged Matteo. 'Di Sione?'

'Yes.' He smiled. 'But you can call me Matteo.'

Abby didn't return the smile.

Instead she blanked him and turned her attention to Pedro, who was climbing into the car.

Was she always this polite with investors? Matteo pondered.

'How long has Pedro been out here?' Matteo enquired, wondering how long he'd had to acclimatise to the hot and humid conditions.

'Long enough,' Abby said and then carried on ignoring him as Pedro started to do some laps.

'Why don't we...?' Matteo started but his voice was drowned out by the sound of the engine and he had to wait till Pedro had passed before continuing. 'Why don't we go somewhere we can talk?'

Still she ignored him and watched the track intently and then, when Pedro had finished a few laps, she turned and finally answered him.

'I don't think so.'

'Sorry?'

'I don't need an investor who wants to pull me away.'

'But Pedro's finished.'

'I'm watching the competition,' she said.

'And you *do* need an investor,' Matteo said.

Not this one, Abby thought.

She knew the Di Sione name, of course she did, and she had looked Matteo up.

Of course she had.

Reckless, wild and debauched, she had read, but looking at the photos of him and finding out a little more about her potential sponsor, it didn't take long for her to work out that he was also as sexy as all hell.

And Abby didn't like sexy.

It terrified her, in fact.

Abby had seen and recognised Matteo the second she had stepped out of the car. He was even better in the flesh and her stomach had curled in a way she would prefer it did not.

She had also seen and felt his eyes roam her body as she had walked towards them and had felt her cheeks turn pink from that fact.

'Can I get earplugs?' Matteo asked. Another team was taking their car out and his hangover was making itself known again. 'I guess we can resort to sign language if we're not allowed to go somewhere decent to talk.'

'Decent?' Abby frowned. What sort of a sponsor was he? Didn't he get that she lived trackside?

She watched Evan put his car through its paces. She had been waiting all day to watch this. Evan Lewis, driver of the Carter team, was one of the Boucher team's toughest opponents. Her friend Bella, who she had studied engineering with, worked for the Carter team and had told Abby that the engine, along with the driver, were poetry in motion. Yes, she had waited all day to see this but as Evan in the aqua-blue car tested the track, she found that she couldn't concentrate.

Matteo stood beside her, swigging from his bottle, which made her thirsty, and as she licked her lips he offered her a drink, as if they had known each other for months.

She gave him a terse shake of her head and he moved forwards and leaned on the rail and bent over a little.

And she noticed.

Oh, she tried to watch Evan but her eyes kept flicking to Matteo's long legs and to a white, slightly crumpled shirt that, despite the heat, wasn't damp. He had a bruise over his left eye and she wanted to know where it had come from. He put down his bottle and in her peripheral vision she saw that he was undoing his shirt.

What the hell?

He turned then and gave her a smile as he popped his hand into the gap he had made in his shirt. 'I've hurt my shoulder,' he briefly explained.

She didn't return his smile, nor did she comment. Instead she walked off.

Matteo had had enough. He'd just have to work out another way to get his grandfather the necklace because if this was the way Abby dealt with sponsors he could just imagine her reaction to him suggesting what she wear to her father's fundraiser!

'Guess what,' he said as he caught up with her. 'You've just lost possibly the most hands-off sponsor you could have ever hoped find...' He looked into the green eyes that would not meet his. 'I'm going. I've decided that I don't want to do business with you. You're rude,' he said and then saw that, just a little, she smiled. 'You're not very nice.'

'I'm not.'

Now she met his eyes and, with contact made, he changed his mind; maybe they could work together after all.

'That's okay,' Matteo said. 'I'll settle for polite.'

Abby gave him an assessing look. She liked it that he had said he'd be hands off—that had been one of the main issues with their previous sponsor; he had demanded so much of Pedro's time. And she liked, too, that Matteo had addressed up front the issue— she'd been rude.

'I can manage polite,' she said.

'Good.' He drained the last of his cola. 'I do need to get something to eat.'

She said something then but it was drowned out by the roar of a car and he couldn't make out the words.

He just watched her mouth.

'I can't hear you,' Matteo said and she had to watch his mouth now. 'Dinner?' he suggested. Finally there was a lull in the noise and he said it again. 'Dinner?'

'Here?' Abby checked and Matteo looked around. The race wasn't till next week and so the corporate caterers weren't here yet.

'Well, I'd prefer a nice lazy meal back at my eight-star hotel but if you insist on here, then I guess it will have to do. Do they have hot dogs in Dubai?'

Abby nodded to a van. 'Not hot dogs exactly...' She took a breath; they were about to talk big business and a takeaway back in the shed really wouldn't cut it. 'When you say your hotel...' She saw him frown, but no, she would make very sure where they would be eating before she agreed to go back to his hotel. 'You do mean the restaurant?'

'What the hell did you think I meant?' Matteo grinned. 'Of course I meant the restaurant. Don't believe everything you read about me, Abby—I'm fast but not that fast.'

She laughed.

Matteo had no idea what a rare sound that was.

'Do you want to meet there?' he suggested, assuming she had a car.

'Sure,' she agreed, and he told her the name of the hotel he was staying at. 'I'll just get changed,' she said, but aware of all she had in her locker she was factoring in a dash back to her own hotel too.

'Please...' He stopped abruptly. Matteo had been about to say, 'Please don't.' She looked amazing in the Boucher green leather after all, but there was something that stopped him and he quickly changed his plea. 'Go ahead,' he said. 'I'll meet you there on the hour.'

Abby felt her cheeks go a little pink again.

'Is it okay if I have a look around before I head off?' he asked.

'Of course.'

One of the mechanics who was peeling a pear offered Matteo half and, when he took it, offered to show him around. It was actually fascinating. There was a whole wall of tyres that would see them through just one race and the science of it all was something Matteo had never considered.

Abby took her time to get ready. Given Matteo had said that they were meeting on the hour there really was no time to go back to her hotel and change. Also, she was incredibly nervous. Oh, she had sat through her share of dinners and lunches, of course, just not with someone as gorgeous as he, and not with someone who made her smile.

Yes, she knew that she came across as brittle at times, but she had been particularly awful to him.

She forgave herself then.

After all, she knew why.

So, what to wear to dinner at an eight-star hotel with a stunning man when you have neither the time nor inclination for a dress but all you have in your locker is a pair of ill-fitting jeans, a massive black T-shirt and flat sandals?

She suppressed a smile because she had known exactly what Matteo had been about to say regarding her leather suit. That was why her cheeks had gone pink. It had felt a little like flirting and Abby wasn't in the least good at that.

She put on some dark glasses and ran a comb through her hair. As she left the locker room she took out her phone to call for a taxi and then startled when she saw that Matteo was still there.

'Sorry, I thought you'd have your own car. Why didn't you say?' he asked.

'I just...' Abby shrugged.

'Come on,' he said and put on his own dark glasses before heading back out in the sun.

What the hell happened there? he thought as they walked to his car. It was as if Abby had done everything possible to look as unattractive as she could. The jeans were massive and as for the T-shirt!

Maybe hot dogs would be a better idea after all.

He glanced down and he didn't think he'd seen an unpainted female toenail before.

Half an hour spent getting ready, for that!

'Will they mind jeans at the hotel?' Abby checked as he drove them there.

'Not the way you wear them.' Matteo turned and smiled. 'You look great.'

Again, she laughed.

'You are such...' She just laughed again. 'I wasn't expecting to go out for dinner, okay? I do know I'm badly dressed.'

'For who?' Matteo shrugged.

He was relaxing to her.

Oh, she was on edge, Abby knew, yet somehow Matteo was relaxing to her.

'What happened to your eye?' she asked.

'I came off a horse,' he said. 'That's how I dislocated my shoulder. I'm supposed to be wearing a shoulder strap.'

'So, why aren't you?'

'I lost it.'

'Oh.'

He was so incredibly handsome and she felt incredibly drab.

'I could stop by my hotel and get changed,' Abby offered, still a little worried that she was way underdressed.

'No need.'

It was, however, Matteo thought, a seriously nice restaurant they were heading to. Seriously, seriously nice but thankfully he'd been here with the sheikh and had lobbed enough tips these past days that he knew they'd give him a welcome smile as they walked in.

But he didn't want her to be uncomfortable.

'We could go to Majlis Al Bahar...' Matteo glanced over and he saw her nervous swallow. 'I'm not getting romantic,' he reassured, because it was possibly the most romantic restaurant on earth. 'It's just that the dress code is more casual and,' he added, 'I kind of want to try it.'

'No,' Abby said. 'The hotel's fine.

So his hotel it was.

'Table for two,' Matteo told the maître d' and such was his confidence that, of course, no one turned a hair and they were shown to their seats.

Her glasses off, those disgusting jeans tucked away, she really was beautiful, Matteo thought. Her eyes were an intense green and thickly lashed and she was the first woman he had ever sat in a restaurant with who wore not a trace of make-up.

He knew what she'd look like in the morning, Matteo thought. Then he reminded himself that he wasn't here for that and so he looked from Abby and out to the view of the Arabian Gulf. 'I love it here,' he admitted. 'I didn't expect to, then again I had no real idea what to expect.'

'I haven't seen much of it,' Abby said. 'We only got here yesterday...'

Matteo was astute enough to frown. 'So how is Pedro doing with the heat?'

She liked that he understood that it mattered.

'A few days more to acclimatise would have been nice,' Abby admitted.

'Is Pedro as temperamental as the press make out?' Matteo asked.

'More so.' She sighed. 'I can't blame him though. He's an amazing talent.'

'You've given him a very early break,' Matteo said, remembering that Pedro had just turned twenty-one and had been nineteen when Abby had taken him on. 'Shouldn't he still be doing the dinky tracks in a go-kart?'

Abby smiled but it was a guarded one. 'He's going to be amazing—he already is.'

He saw her tight smile and read it.

Someone with a far bigger cash pot would snap him up very soon.

'Treat him like a star, then,' Matteo said. 'Make him never want to leave.' He saw the set of her lips. 'What's his latest gripe?' he asked and her mouth relaxed into a soft laugh at his perception.

'Well, some of the other drivers have suites with their own gym and lap pool.' She looked at Matteo, who said nothing. 'These guys are incredibly fit. You have to be to race at that speed. I know how taxing it is just doing a few gentle laps.'

'It didn't look particularly gentle to me,' Matteo said. 'So, what's it like?' he asked. 'Driving one?'

And she knew the line the guys used but that would really tip her into flirting with him.

'It's amazing,' she said, instead of saying that it was better than sex.

It had to be.

Her one experience had been hell after all.

No, she would not be flirting.

'Pedro doesn't like using the hotel pool and gym,' Abby said. 'And I get that, I do, but…' She loathed talking about money, but that was what they were here to do. 'Our budget's tight.'

'And Pedro doesn't want to hear that?'

'He's been really good,' Abby said. 'They all have been. It's hard watching the others swan off to fancy restaurants when we're heading for the burger bar.

We all want better things and know that we have to work for it. It's just hard juggling egos. And also I know that Pedro's right—he'd do better with more resources and I'd do better if I had more time to focus on the car and the opposition.'

'Instead of playing bookkeeper?' Matteo asked and she gave a low laugh.

'And PA, and travel agent…'

'I get it.'

How could he? 'How come you want to invest?' she asked him.

'Well, I think you're going places,' Matteo said. 'And I want to be securely on board when you do. I have a thing for outside chances.' He looked at the wine menu. 'What are we drinking?' Matteo asked.

'Water for me…'

'You're a cheap date.'

'This isn't a date, Matteo,' she said.

'Actually, no, it isn't.' He put down the menu and was serious. He was interested in sponsoring the team. Seriously so. Matteo was a gambler by nature but this was a huge one. He wasn't thinking about the necklace or her father now. Matteo's head was in the game and if he was going to be a sponsor, then there had to be rules. 'My relationships run into hours rather than days. Believe me, you don't want to know…'

'I already do!' she said.

'Which means, if we want this to work, then it's hands off each other.'

'I'm good with that,' she said.

'Anyway,' Matteo added, 'I don't date.'

'And I don't drink.'

'At all?'

'Nope.' She shook her head.

'Ever?'

'Never.' She smiled at his curiosity. 'Well, I tried it and didn't like it.'

'Okay, water for two it is.'

'You can.'

'I know that I can,' Matteo said, 'but I'm keeping my wits about me with you.'

He looked at the menu and groaned. 'Truffle-crusted scallops—I know what I'm having.'

His groan made her stomach tighten; the low sound of his want caused her breath to hold in her throat, and then he looked up.

His eyes were the darkest navy and when he smiled so, too, did she.

'That's better,' Matteo said.

He was nice, her heart said.

Just that.

The food was amazing and the company too, and he really did take her concerns seriously.

'I had a sponsor last year, not a particularly generous one,' Abby explained. 'He rang all the time, wanted constant progress reports. Race day was hell.

He wanted me to join him and his cronies for a champagne brunch and Pedro to be sociable...'

'Look, I get you don't want someone sticking their nose in and I can manage lunch by myself. And, for what it's worth, I won't be putting pressure on you or your team. I wouldn't expect much this year...'

'Oh, no,' Abby interrupted. 'We're winning the Henley Cup this year.'

'I'm just saying that I'm patient.'

'Pedro will be off soon,' Abby said. 'He's a rising star and someone will make an offer that I can't match any day soon.'

'Probably.' Matteo nodded. He'd thought the same but now he could really see the problem. 'Hunter's retiring at the end of this year and I guess the Lachance team...' He paused, remembering that Abby had briefly dated him. 'Hey, didn't you two...?'

'We're winning this year,' Abby said, not answering the question. 'I want the Henley Cup—Dubai first, then Italy, then Monte Carlo.'

'Then you need to keep your driver happy,' Matteo said. 'How tight is it?' he asked.

No one knew just how bad it was and Abby was extremely reluctant to tell him.

Matteo watched as she fiddled with her glass. 'The only thing I want in a relationship is honesty,' he said and then he started to laugh. 'I only get to use that line in business.'

Even Abby laughed.

'So, how about we be honest with each other? Whatever you tell me goes no further than here, whatever we then decide.'

She believed him. And, Abby thought, maybe it would be a relief to tell someone the truth.

No one knew just how bad it was.

Her team all thought she was particularly tense; they didn't know that she was waking up in dread every night. Abby was even considering agreeing to her father's ridiculous bribe to go along to his fund-raiser just for the injection of cash he had promised if she did.

The very thought of that made her sick.

She wondered if the photograph of her and Hunter still hung on her father's study wall.

Abby closed her eyes for a second, as panic briefly hit.

No, she would not be going cap in hand to her father.

She opened her eyes to Matteo's waiting ones and decided to tell him the truth.

'I can't get us to Italy.'

Matteo said nothing.

'I've got the car and equipment covered but I can't get the team there.'

'The money's run out?'

Abby nodded.

He didn't get up and walk off and he didn't berate. He just sat there.

Thinking.

Then he gave in on water and called for a large cognac.

And still he sat there thinking.

Not about the necklace that he was supposed to be here for; instead he was thinking about cars and a team and it gave him a buzz that had been missing at the casino of late. He didn't like motor racing. Fast cars were the only vice he didn't have. There were too many painful memories attached.

Yet, he was starting to come around.

Watching Abby and later Pedro putting the car through its paces, speaking with the mechanics, gauging the opposition...

There was an attraction to the sport that Matteo had never anticipated when he had taken the challenge on.

He asked for figures and she went red in the neck but told him, and she watched as he crunched a few numbers on a calculator.

Not his phone, she noted.

And it wasn't a two-dollar calculator either.

He had beautiful hands, Abby thought, and she liked the way his tongue popped out as he concentrated.

Matteo knew he should conclude this meeting now. The type of money that was required here outweighed the necklace and there was practically a guarantee of zero return.

'Why do you think you're a chance?' he asked.

'I built the car,' Abby said. 'I have the most fear-less driver I've ever seen. Pedro's a bit raw but that's good. He's unpredictable. No one except for me—actually, not even me—knows what he's capable of...'

Still Matteo looked.

'But he needs the right tool and my car is that.'

Still he looked. His face gave away nothing, Abby thought, but he had demanded honesty and if that was the case there was something rather large that she was leaving out.

'And I've been waiting nine years for this.'

She didn't tell him why; she just told him that she had.

He saw something then and its name was deter-mination.

No, the numbers might not add up but the feeling in his gut tipped the scale.

'Tell you what,' Matteo finally said and Abby found she was holding her breath. 'If you can come in in the top five here in Dubai, then I'll take care of getting the team to Italy.'

'Will you be staying to watch?'

'God, yes,' Matteo said. 'And sorry if you don't like it but if you do place, then I'll be in Italy too. Don't worry though. I shan't be breathing down your neck.'

And for the first time, possibly ever, Abby imagined just that—a man breathing down her neck, or even *on* her neck…

Not just any man.

Him.

He expected her to backtrack, to maybe push for a lower place, but instead she looked straight back at him.

'We're going to do better than fifth.'

He really, really hoped so.

And so, too, did she.

'Right,' Matteo said and called for the bill and then he asked for her bank details.

'We haven't placed yet.'

'I'm just making sure that you do.'

He paid and then asked for a driver to take her back to her hotel. 'My sister Allegra has got a big charity event tomorrow. I think we should go.'

'You said…' Abby started but Matteo overrode her.

'Everyone will be there, including the press. It might rattle the opposition if they think you've got a Di Sione on board.' He tapped the side of his head. 'Mind games.'

Oh, it would seriously rattle the opposition and Abby would take any edge that she could get.

She thought of Hunter and that terrible night and she *had* to beat him this year.

It was her only chance for revenge.

'Abby, you need to ooze confidence,' Matteo said. 'Doesn't matter how you feel on the inside.'

'Please.' She rolled her eyes. 'It's easy for you...'

'You don't know me,' Matteo interrupted. 'But believe me when I say, never let them smell fear.'

She nodded.

'So will you come?' he asked.

'Yes.'

'Good,' Matteo said. 'After tomorrow I'll leave you alone to do your thing. If I send a car for you at ten would that be okay?'

'There's no need for that. I'll meet you here.'

'Sure.'

When her car arrived it was Matteo, rather than the driver, who opened the door for her, and they spoke for a moment before she got in.

'I'll see you tomorrow,' he said and she nodded and then he shook her hand. 'And you need to dress up.'

'Excuse me?' she flared.

'I don't care what you wear in your down time,' Matteo said. 'But if you want to wear the Di Sione name on your car and your overalls, then you have to look the part when we're out.'

'And I thought brunch on race day was an imposition...' She was about to tell him to get stuffed but not only couldn't Abby afford to, she didn't want to either. He was right; if her team were going to get anywhere, then maybe it was time to play the corporate game a touch and maybe she could do that with him.

He hadn't turned a hair at her jeans; he had made her feel relaxed and comfortable as she had told him the terrible mess she was in.

'Tomorrow is work,' he said as Abby climbed into the car but then, just before he closed the door, he gave her that smile. 'Not that we can't enjoy ourselves while working.'

The car drove off and Abby found her heart was thumping. They had very carefully laid the ground rules at the table—they were completely hands off, she knew that.

Matteo's inference had been that they would simply enjoy provoking the press and the opposition.

It was her own imagination that was for the first time, if not exactly running wild, then peeking out and blinking at the sun.

A dark sun named Matteo Di Sione.

CHAPTER THREE

ABBY DIDN'T SLEEP WELL.

Yes, their conversation last night about money should have reassured her but Abby knew that she'd lied to Matteo.

They didn't really have a hope of making fifth place.

But they had to though.

Not just for the chance of Matteo investing in them.

Her breakfast was delivered and Abby decided to eat it in bed and, as she did, she took out her laptop and read the news.

The sports news, of course.

The Boucher team barely got a mention.

The Carter team were on form, she read, and the Lachance team got plenty of mentions too.

Or rather Hunter did.

She looked at him, dressed in his familiar yellow leather and wearing that cocky, arrogant smile, and if there was such a thing as pure hate, then Abby felt that now.

She wasn't scared of him any more.

It had been nine years since that terrible night and now, instead of scared, she was angry.

And it was such an undiluted, white-hot anger that ravaged her that it required revenge.

Hunter was thirty-four now and, to date, the Henley cup had been his for nine of the past ten years.

The one year that he had lost it had been the night that Abby had chosen to end their brief relationship.

Foolish timing perhaps but she had arrived in Monte Carlo and had sat in a hotel room, knowing their time together had ended.

They had only been going out for four weeks but Hunter wanted to move things along.

He'd invited her to Monte Carlo.

There would be separate hotel rooms, Hunter had assured her, given he needed his space before a race, but Abby knew very well what was going to come after.

She had gone on the pill but even as she had flown there, Abby had known that the nerves she felt weren't the ones you should be feeling when you were about to lose your virginity.

Hunter made her feel nervous, in a way that she couldn't quite define.

It had been cars that that had drawn them together at first but it hadn't taken long to realise he didn't want a discussion.

Hunter talked and she was supposed to listen.

Everything she had said about cars he had dismissed.

Oh, at eighteen, who wouldn't be flattered to be going out with a star and to be picked up and whisked off to Monte Carlo in his private jet?

Only the gloss had already worn off by then.

Abby hadn't wanted to go but her father had been appalled when she'd suggested cancelling.

Hunter's jet was already on the way!

And so, Abby had gone. She had had a few drinks for courage during the race and then back at the hotel, as Hunter had faced the press after his surprise loss, Abby had had a couple more.

He had phoned and said that he was back at the hotel and Abby had taken the elevator up to Hunter's room to tell him that no, she didn't want to go out tonight and neither did she want to stay in.

In fact, Abby had already booked a ticket and was flying home to New York that night.

As her father had later pointed out—you don't tell a man who has just lost a cup that you're breaking up with him.

So what? Abby had thought at the time.

She hadn't wanted to sleep with him and if she'd stayed, then she knew how the night was expected to end. Abby didn't want her first to be Hunter; it had been as simple as that.

And, her father had also added, Hunter's lawyers

would make mincemeat out of her, given that she'd gone to his hotel room after all.

Drunk.

'Not drunk, Dad, I was just...' But then she had stopped trying to describe how she had felt that night as she'd knocked on his hotel door.

Abby couldn't really remember how she had felt before it happened.

She simply couldn't remember who the woman was that had stepped into a man's hotel suite and expected to be able to speak her mind.

Which she had.

They were over, Abby had told him.

'Not quite,' Hunter said.

She hadn't fought enough, according to her father. There wasn't a scratch on Hunter after all.

Abby had frozen when first he had grabbed her and then she had tried to run but had only made it a few steps across his suite and he had pushed her into the bathroom.

And when *it* was over, when she lay on a cold bathroom floor and thought she could not be more broken both inside or out, Hunter had stood and then urinated over her.

Just to be sure.

Absolutely he had broken her.

Not now.

'I'll take that cup from you,' Abby vowed and spoke to the screen. 'You'll go out the loser you really are.'

Matteo was right: it was all about mind games.

Today Hunter and the other teams would find out that Matteo Di Sione was considering coming on board.

And that would rattle them.

The Di Sione empire was amazing—from shipping, to apps, to computers, they had their hand in everything and had money everywhere.

Matteo was right again: she needed to ooze confidence, not dread.

Maybe now was not the time to be spending money on clothes when she was worried about the hotel bill but there were slim pickings in her wardrobe.

There was a dress that might have been handy for dinner yesterday but wasn't suitable for a gala event.

And then there was the dress that Abby had sworn she would wear if they ever made it to the podium.

It was sexy; it was the colour of tarnished silver with a slight green hue and just way too much for today.

Truth be known, Abby could never see herself having the confidence to wear it—wherever they placed.

She knew that she would have to buy something for today.

Abby signed into her bank account and blinked when she saw the balance.

Oh, my God!

Matteo had meant what he said about ensuring they had every chance of winning.

Nervous, excited and more than a little bit relieved, instead of quickly dressing and hitting the shops Abby dealt with serious business first and rang down to Reception. Having made the necessary arrangements, she called Pedro.

'Hi,' Abby said when he picked up.

'Abby, I don't have time to talk.' Pedro's tone was clipped. 'I am just going down to the pool and then I'm hitting the gym.'

'About that,' Abby said. 'Pedro, I've just spoken with Reception and you're being moved to a suite with its own lap pool and gym.'

'You're serious?'

'I am. Someone's already on their way to move your things.'

'Abby, thanks,' Pedro said. 'This will really help with my training.'

'Good.'

It seemed like an unnecessary luxury, but Abby knew that it wasn't. The facilities in Dubai were stunning and she knew only too well that the other top teams would be utilizing them. Pedro would be out running in the midday heat. He would do everything he could to get his body prepared for the race and so it was very nice to be able to give him this.

Now she could concentrate on getting ready for today.

The shopping in Dubai was supposed to be amazing too but Abby really didn't have the time or the inclination to explore. There were, though, some boutiques on the ground floor of the hotel and one had caught her eye when they checked in.

It wasn't one of the famous international designers; instead it was a niche boutique from a local designer and tentatively Abby stepped inside.

The dresses were exquisite and, when the assistant found out where she was going today, she took Abby under her wing.

Abby had studied fashion for a year; she could mentally dress anyone so long as it wasn't herself. Even though she had been pushed into it by her father, Abby had vaguely enjoyed it and knew what she liked—and understated was it!

'This one,' the assistant said, holding up a dress in pale coral. It was a very sheer fabric with a slip dress beneath and it was very feminine and floaty and really not the sort of thing Abby would choose.

'What about this,' Abby suggested and held up a similar dress in grey, but the assistant shook her head.

'Try the coral one on.'

Oh, Abby hated this.

It felt as if she was dressing up for a family photo, she thought as she stepped into a large changing room. But reminding herself it was business, she put the dress on.

'You look very elegant,' the assistant said after she had asked Abby if she could see it on.

'It's a bit much.' Abby shook her head, thinking of it with high heels, but the assistant was far more used to this type of thing and disappeared.

'Try these,' she said when she returned and handed Abby a pair of flat strappy sandals. They were thin jewelled straps and yet somehow very neutral, and when she tried them on the assistant was right—the dress looked more sophisticated than it would with high heels.

'I like it,' Abby admitted.

'You need to get your hair smoothed out and then tied back,' the assistant said and, remembering Matteo's comments last night, Abby wondered if people in Dubai just spoke their mind.

'I really don't have time to get my hair done,' Abby said, given that it was well after nine.

'I can ring over to the salon,' the assistant pushed, 'if you are pressed for time.'

'Sure.' Abby gave a tight smile as she paid.

She then went into the hairdresser's and had her hair smoothed and there she bought a lipstick that would go better with the dress.

Abby didn't have time to be nervous; she was far too late for Matteo for that. But even so, she managed to be as she stepped into his hotel and saw him waiting in the foyer.

'Wow!' he said. 'You're worth the wait.'

Somehow he both welcomed her and told her off for keeping him waiting.

'We need to get going,' Matteo said.

He really had no idea of the effort she had gone to in order to get her looking like this and Abby kind of liked that about him.

Still, she wasn't so much nervous as they walked to the car; rather she was incredibly aware, not of her unfamiliar attire, more of the man she was with.

Very, very aware.

That was the best way she could describe it.

She was aware of the dry warmth of his hand on her arm as he led her to the waiting car.

And aware of him as he stretched out beside her and then popped a couple of painkillers and took them without water.

'Do you have a headache?' Abby asked, guessing he must have hit the clubs after he had dropped her off last night.

'My shoulder,' Matteo said.

'You should have worn the sling.'

'I know.' He just shrugged and obviously it hurt to do so because he winced, but then he turned the conversation to work as the car moved through the magnificent streets. 'How's Pedro?'

'He's being moved to a better suite as we speak,' Abby said. 'He's much happier than he was this time yesterday.'

'And if Pedro's happy, we're all happy.'

'Thank you,' Abby said. 'Whether or not it makes a difference…'

'Oh, it will make a difference,' Matteo interrupted but then he saw the anxious dart of her eyes and guessed she was worrying what would happen if they didn't place fifth. 'Just enjoy the buildup to the race,' Matteo said. 'We'll see what happens on race day and then we'll speak after.'

The charity gala that his sister had organised was a huge event and must have taken a lot of work to plan.

There were beautiful people everywhere and no, Abby didn't feel overdressed now; in fact, she was very relieved that she hadn't gone for grey.

It was just such a beautiful summery day and they headed off to find his sister.

'What's she like?' Abby asked.

'Who, Allegra?' Matteo checked and rolled his eyes. 'She's a goody-two-shoes. Don't mention to her that I've hurt my shoulder.'

'Why not?'

'She'll worry,' Matteo said. 'There she is.'

He called out and waved with his good arm, and an attractive woman came over and they greeted each other with a kiss on the cheek. 'This is Abby,' Matteo said. 'My latest venture.'

'Matteo,' Allegra scolded.

'Business venture.' Matteo grinned. 'How are you?'

'Busy,' Allegra admitted. 'What have you done to your eye?'

'I just knocked into a door.'

'I don't believe you for a moment,' Allegra said. 'And I can't believe you've been here for more than a week and I haven't seen you.'

'Well, you had this to arrange.'

'It's been crazy...' Allegra admitted but didn't finish her sentence—someone was calling out to her and she gave Matteo and Abby an apologetic smile. 'I really would love to stop and speak but I think it's going to have to be later.'

'Allegra,' Matteo said. 'I need to speak to you about Grandfather.'

'Now?'

He nodded and Abby saw that his expression was completely serious. 'He's not doing too well.'

'I know that,' Allegra said. 'Bianca and I have already spoken to him.'

'I think you need to take some time and go and see him,' Matteo said. Allegra closed her eyes and it was clear that she was upset.

'I know he's not well but...'

'Come on,' Matteo said to his sister and he took her by the elbow. 'I won't be a moment,' he said to Abby as he led Allegra somewhere a little more private. Abby tried not to watch but she glanced over once and saw Allegra put her hand on Matteo's shoulder and give it a squeeze.

His sore shoulder.

Oh, poor Matteo!

He didn't wince; Matteo just took Allegra's hand from his shoulder and gently let it go.

They were far from gushing with each other but Abby could tell, even from this distance, that they cared about what was being discussed.

It was so different from her family.

Annabel and Abby could go months without so much as a brief catch-up, and as for Abby and her father...

Maybe she should make the effort, Abby thought.

Yes, he had hurt her a lot when she had told him about Hunter's attack but, trying to be fair to her father, though he hadn't handled it well, maybe he had been grieving.

Never more than at that time had Abby wanted her mother, but she had been dead for three years by then.

Perhaps it was time to try and be family again?

She jumped a little as Matteo came back to her side.

'Sorry about that,' Matteo said. 'Allegra already knows that my grandfather is ill but I don't think she knew just how bad things have got.'

'Is he very sick?'

Matteo nodded and for a moment, just a brief moment, he looked at Abby and wondered if he could tell her about the necklace and the real reason that he had made contact.

It almost felt as if he could.

But then he remembered the brittle woman he had met yesterday and decided that no, it was far too risky to chance it.

He was here for the team; he really was. There was no need to confuse things by bringing up the necklace just yet.

All that could wait.

'Come on…' Matteo said.

'Where?'

'To the sky.'

There were helicopter rides and he took her on one, and Abby, who apart from the racetrack had only seen one restaurant and one boutique during her time in Dubai, was treated to a bird's-eye view.

Over the artificial Palm Islands they flew and Abby had never seen anything more stunning. And she also saw where Matteo had suggested they go to dinner. The city seemed to glitter gold and silver and they flew, too, over the racetrack where the first leg of the Henley Cup would be held.

This time next week, she'd be down there, Abby thought with a flurry of both nerves and excitement.

They stepped off the helicopter and Abby took a moment more than Matteo did to find her land legs.

'It makes you dizzy, doesn't it,' Matteo said. 'Let's go and find something to eat.'

They didn't have to look very far; there was plenty to choose from, and though they had lunch it was a quick one because, as Matteo leafed through a glossy program, he decided that he wanted to look at the racehorses that were being paraded.

'Oh, look at that one…' Abby said. It was a stunning, white, purebred Arabian stallion, so highly strung that he looked as if at any moment he might take off.

'Bastard!' Matteo said but didn't get a chance to explain as someone tapped him on his shoulder.

The sore one.

'Kedah!' Matteo grinned as he turned around and saw who it was and he introduced them both. 'Abby, this is Kedah. We studied briefly together in New York.'

'Until you dropped out.'

'I'm still standing,' Matteo said. 'And this is Abby, owner and manager of the Boucher racing team.'

'It is very nice to meet you,' Sheikh Kedah said. He was incredibly handsome, Abby thought. He was beautifully presented, dressed in a robe of pale gold with a *keffiyah* tied and skilfully draped but he had that same wild gleam in his eye as Matteo and they made an extremely good-looking pair. Abby could only imagine the sort of trouble these two got into. 'Your driver did well here last year. Fifth, if I remember rightly?'

Abby nodded, surprised that he knew and pleasantly surprised also that Kedah didn't mention that, after that race, Pedro had gone on to place nowhere.

Kedah turned to Matteo. 'How is the shoulder?'

'Still sore.' Matteo smiled. 'Black and blue...'

'The doctor said you would bruise.' Kedah nodded. 'So do you still want him even after he threw you?'

'Absolutely,' Matteo said and then looked back to the stallion. 'Abby and I were just admiring him.'

At ten minutes to three, two thoughts hit and both unsettled her.

That the horse Matteo had fallen off was a thoroughbred racehorse. What the hell would have possessed him to be riding that?

But she couldn't dwell on it because another thought was invading.

She wanted to see his shoulder.

Abby, who just pushed down all thoughts of sex, who actually felt sick at the thought of intimacy, suddenly wanted to go back to the hotel and peel off his shirt and touch that bruised skin.

With her mouth.

'Are you okay?' Matteo checked, picking up on the sudden tension in her.

'Sorry?'

'Kedah was just saying he'd love to come to the race...'

'Oh!'

'We're not allowed to talk to Abby on race day though,' Matteo warned him.

'I'd love to be there,' Kedah said to Abby and then addressed Matteo. 'If the Boucher team make the podium, you get the horse,' the sheikh said and they shook hands.

'Do you bet on everything?' Abby asked when Kedah had gone.

'Not everything,' Matteo said and then he met her eyes and again stopped what he was about to say.

He'd never have put money on enjoying today.

Usually, often, always, he'd be bored by now and would have run out of things to say.

Usually, often, always, he'd be glancing at his phone and wondering if they went back to the hotel now and slept together, then he could drop her back and hit the town with Kedah.

Usually, often, always, he'd have said hi to his sister, stayed for half an hour and then said goodbye.

Instead today felt like the best of days and there was but one reason why.

'What the hell were you doing riding him?' Abby asked, tearing her eyes from his gaze and looking back to the magnificent stallion. 'Do you ride?'

'Not really,' Matteo admitted.

'When you say "not really…"?' Abby checked.

'No.'

'You could have been killed,' Abby said and she was far from joking. This beast would test the limits of the most experienced rider. 'Why would you take such a risk?'

'Do you say the same to Pedro when he stands on the gas?'

'Pedro's skilled and trained,' Abby retorted. 'You're a bit tall to be a jockey.'

Her cheeks were that lovely shade of turned-on pink, Matteo thought, and he was quite sure that it had nothing to do with the sun.

He wanted to turn her around and speak into her ear and put on a high voice, just to make her laugh as he told her what a *fabulous* jockey he was. And then Matteo wanted to be warned that public displays of affection could not happen here.

And then...

'Come on,' Matteo said. 'The fashion show's starting. You used...' He faltered; it had been her father who had told him that she'd once studied fashion.

'Used to what?'

'I thought I read somewhere that you used to study fashion?'

'I did,' Abby said. 'Where did you hear that?'

'I can't remember.' Matteo shrugged. 'I must have come across it when I was researching the team.'

He'd lied.

Matteo sat there beside her and he knew he'd lied, only not in the same way that he had to his sister— that had been about protecting Allegra, this had been about protecting himself.

It didn't matter, Matteo told himself.

He and Abby weren't going anywhere.

Even if they slept together, and from the heat between them that was becoming increasingly likely, he knew that they wouldn't last.

Matteo meant it—he would never get close to another.

Abby didn't notice the silence. It was actually so nice to be away from cars and she had never felt like that. Cars were both her work and her hobby but it was just nice to take a day off, but more than that, she knew it was because of Matteo.

They watched the fashion show and every second model who walked out onto the runway Matteo said, 'You'd look good in that.'

And then out came the underwear and he made no comment.

Not one.

They were both trying so hard to behave and, for Abby, to even have to *try* to behave was a revelation.

Finally, with the fashion show over they decided to call it a day.

'I just want to say goodbye to Allegra...'

'Go,' Abby said.

'Thanks.'

He appreciated it.

She wasn't needy and he liked that.

He liked her.

As they sat in the car on the way back to her hotel, he handed her his phone and Abby looked at a photo of the two of them, both laughing as they sat watching the fashion show.

Neither with a care in the world, it would seem.

Business or Romance? the headline said.

'Oh, no,' Abby wailed. 'Why would they jump to that?'

'Don't worry about it.' Matteo shrugged.

'But we want them to think…'

'Oh, they'll be thinking,' he said.

The car pulled up at her hotel and Abby wondered if he'd suggest dinner and she wondered if she might accept.

But Matteo, being Matteo, skipped entrée, main and dessert and, after such a lovely day, for him the ending was inevitable.

'We could,' Matteo said, 'always go to mine.'

That delicious mouth moved in for the kill and what startled Abby the most was that she wanted to accept, to just close her eyes and give in to the bliss he offered, except she jerked her head back.

'I'm assuming we're not talking about the restaurant at your hotel?'

'We're not.'

For Matteo sex was as straightforward and as simple as that.

'What happened to keeping it strictly business?' Abby asked.

'I can juggle both.'

He looked into green eyes that had been relaxed and smiling all day but now had turned to sleet.

'I'll see you on race day.' Abby's voice was tart—

he could feel her anger and indignation emanating—
and Matteo, who only ever played with the willing,
leant back. 'If you're still interested, that is.' She
didn't wait for the driver to open the door for her;
instead she got out and slammed the door shut.

You're not here to seduce, Matteo reminded himself as the driver took his rarely rejected passenger
back to his hotel.

Matteo never misread signs.

Today the two of them had blasted a heat to rival
a Dubai sun.

It was better this way, he conceded as he climbed
out of the car and headed to his luxury suite.

If ever he'd been glad that he hadn't told Abby
about the origins of them, then it was now, because
he was seriously interested in the Boucher team.

And, far more worryingly for Matteo, he was also
seriously interested in Abby herself.

Which was, for a die-hard bachelor, very troubling indeed.

He was now terribly glad that Abby had said no.

CHAPTER FOUR

How HAD HE ever lived his life without this? Matteo wondered when racing day dawned.

It made the casino look like a playground.

The noise, the crowd, the scent, just the complete buzz was made all the better for having a stake in it, Matteo thought as he made his way to the Boucher shed.

He wondered as to his reception but soon found out he needn't have.

It was quite refreshing to have no one remotely interested in him.

Pedro was playing video games and just blocking out everyone as he did what he had to do to get himself into the zone. Abby, dressed like some man in bottle-green trousers and top, with a baseball cap on, was doing some last-minute checks on the computer. The team were working on the car and Matteo knew when to stay back.

Of course she noticed him.

Abby had been wondering all week if she'd blown

her chance with an amazing sponsor. Absolutely she knew she had been giving out mixed signals the entire time they spent together.

Matteo just didn't need to know why.

Yes, it was a relief to see him and an even bigger relief when he left without demanding an update or even a minute of anyone's time.

Matteo and Kedah went for lunch and then placed their bets. Matteo decided to bet on the Boucher team placing. But then, as the cars all took up their positions, and just before betting closed, just for the hell of it, Matteo placed a ridiculous amount on a win.

Dubai had turned it on and as the cars took off, the roar that went up combined with the engines and there was a new love in Matteo's life.

Motor racing.

He looked to Abby; she was lost to him for the next couple of hours, her focus on the race, and Matteo was fine with that.

He'd apologise later, he decided, glad that she had drawn the line.

He could understand now her obsession with the sport. *Neck and neck* took on a whole new meaning when it went for two hours and Abby never broke her focus, not once.

They were going to place, Matteo thought as he glanced at the times and the top four came into the second-last lap.

Better than that, they might hit the podium.

Pedro overtook Evan just as they came into the final lap. The Boucher team was a split second behind Lachance. Pedro was biting at Hunter's heels though, just waiting for that chance to take him.

And then, when Hunter refused to give him that chance, Pedro made his own.

Young, brave and foolish, at the final turn he took Hunter!

The roar from the Boucher team drowned the engines, and even Abby stopped working. There was nothing she could do from here except scream her lungs out.

Pedro gunned it.

He simply took the engine that she had designed, the car that she had built, the driver that she had nurtured and the team that should lose right into the history books, and Abby just stood there screaming as Pedro took her baby home.

They had won!

Not only that, Evan had overtaken Hunter, who had struggled to right his car from Pedro's brave manoeuvre.

The noise was deafening but all Abby could hear was silence.

She was being thumped on the back, lifted up; she was screaming but she could not feel or hear a thing.

And then she saw Matteo, right there in front of her.

For the first time today, she properly saw him.

He was wearing black jeans and a black shirt. Dark, dangerous and unshaven, the only safe thing about him was that those full blood-red lips were smiling.

At her.

'You did it,' he said, moving that final step into her space so that his voice was all she could hear.

Matteo didn't even get what she had done—that she had finally beaten Hunter—but right now she didn't even care about that.

'I'm sorry about the other night,' he said, his eyes intent on hers.

'I am too,' Abby admitted, to her own surprise.

Elation enabled honesty and with those words she admitted the truth she dared not, even to herself—she was sorry that she had said no.

And then there was no space between them. They were wrapped in each other's arms and the mouth she had wanted from the night they had met was on hers, crushing hers. Had she imagined a kiss over the years it had always been a gentle one.

This was not that.

It was consuming, blatant and very fierce and, unthinking, her mouth opened in delicious reflex. His tongue was straight in, and yet she, too, sought his, like some exotic sword fight, where both were winners as they partook in the deepest, sexiest kiss.

God, he was shameless, Abby thought. He removed her cap and his hand pressed her head further in so she could feel the skin shredding on her jaw. Then he took the energy of their kiss and didn't just sustain it; Matteo heightened it. He was hard and pressing into her and she could feel every delicious inch. His hands were now travelling down to her bottom and pulling her into him. Yet, rather than pull back, Abby was just as on fire and as sexed up as he.

And then they remembered the rules and pulled their mouths rather than their bodies back.

'When we win...we kiss...' Matteo said.

She could live with that.

They were breathing so hard just staring at each other.

'When we place, we kiss,' he said, kissing her cheek as if it were her mouth and that made her laugh. 'And if we lose,' he continued, making out with her ear, 'then we have to commiserate...'

He was still hard and still there, nudging her stomach, and there was the beautiful absence of fear, even when he pulled back and looked right into her eyes.

'What does it feel like to win?' Matteo asked.

'Better than sex,' Abby said, no longer scared to throw a flirty line.

And she expected him to laugh or to haul her closer in for more of a feel of his erection but instead he looked deeper into her eyes.

'Then someone hasn't been doing you right,' Matteo said.

He intended to remedy that later tonight.

CHAPTER FIVE

HUNTER SAW THEM.

He got out of his car and looked over and saw the woman he had left lying bruised and bleeding on a marble bathroom floor, and then pissed all over, now happy and free.

'Whoa!' The reporters shouted in several languages as Hunter kicked his car and threw his helmet down to the ground and then stormed off.

Abby and Matteo didn't see a thing.

They were too busy laughing as Kedah informed them that Matteo was now the owner of an extremely temperamental horse!

'Her name is Abby,' Matteo said but she deliberately missed the inference.

'I'm not temperamental.'

Or maybe she was, because Abby, who didn't cry, almost did when she watched as Pedro stood in first place on the podium.

'I almost want a glass of champagne,' Abby admitted as Pedro sprayed the crowd with the same.

The Carter team was in second place and Evan grinned and waved and took the dousing.

Hunter attempted to do the same.

It was a good day.

A brilliant day.

And the world was waiting for the press conference.

Oh, they were an arrogant lot, Matteo thought as the drivers came in and took their seats.

Pedro sat there grinning; so, too, did Evan. Even Hunter had recovered from his hissy fit and that assured smile was back on his face.

'I have to congratulate Pedro…' They were the first words out of Hunter's mouth.

He was charming, said a reporter standing to the side of Matteo and Abby.

'Narcissists generally are,' Matteo drawled.

He didn't like him.

'I lost my focus for a second,' Hunter conceded, 'and Pedro took his chance.'

Hunter made it sound like he had lost rather than that they had won and Matteo felt Abby tense beside him.

'Don't worry about him,' Matteo said, without looking over to her. 'You know you won.' He then listened as a reporter asked Hunter a question.

'What about your reaction after the race? You seemed pretty angry.'

'Ha.' Hunter shrugged and then spread his hands,

holding his palm to the sky. 'I guess I'm not used to it...' And then he put down his hands and looked straight over to Matteo as he spoke on. 'I tend to get there first.'

Matteo didn't know that he had hackles till then, yet he felt them rise and he watched as Hunter's gaze moved to the woman who stood beside him.

'That was for me...' Abby said and Matteo frowned because her voice was slurred.

His newly discovered hackles were still up and Matteo put an arm around Abby.

'It's okay.' He didn't know what was going on but he could feel Abby's distress and he tried to re-assure her.

But all she could hear was *Wah-wah-wah*...

The rest of what Matteo said she lost.

There was a roaring in Abby's ears and her chest felt closed and she could feel that her lips were tingling.

'I can't breathe...' she gasped.

'Abby...' Matteo said, but then she lost track of his deep smoky voice again and she made one last desperate plea.

'Don't let Hunter see me like this.'

Matteo got her out of the press conference and to a horrid plastic seat, where he sat her down and told her to cup her hands over her face. 'You're having a panic attack.'

He was just calm.

On the outside.

Matteo never let anyone glimpse his fear.

He went over to a guy who was walking past and tipped the man's burger into his hand and returned to Abby with the paper bag. 'Breathe into this…' Matteo said and he just kept on talking in his lovely deep voice and telling her she would soon be okay. 'It will pass soon,' he assured. 'My sister Natalia gets them and they pass. I promise.'

He just sat with her the entire way through it. Abby was sweating and white and her eyes were wide open and looking into his as she breathed in and out of the paper bag and then moved it aside.

'He lost,' Abby said and, with a sinking feeling, Matteo knew, he just knew, that they weren't talking about Hunter losing the race today.

Matteo felt sick; he actually did but he just looked back at her.

'He lost a race…' Abby said. She could not do it in full sentences. 'I was ending it. We'd only gone out a few times. We'd never…'

And he didn't know what to say.

'He got so angry.'

Matteo just didn't know what to say.

'I told my father. He said not to report it.' She shook her head. 'You see, I was drunk…'

And now Matteo did know what to say.

It was his first rule.

'Then he should have seen you safely home.'

'I was in his hotel room.'

No, he would not let her go there.

'Then he should have checked into another or put you to bed and slept in the chair,' Matteo said. 'There's no excuse for what he did.'

'It was *so* violent.' Abby relived it just for a second and she watched Matteo blink, not once but three times, and then he responded.

'He should have treated you like glass,' Matteo said.

'It was my first time...'

'Crystal glass, then,' Matteo amended. 'And that was *not* your first time—that's not sex.'

'It's the only sex I know.'

And then her panic came back because they were coming out of the press conference. 'He can't see me like this.'

Yet she couldn't stand.

'What if we look like we were having an intimate moment—is that okay?' Matteo gently checked and she nodded.

He just wrapped her in his arms and she saw the yellow leather of Hunter walking past and she heard the increasing *thud, thud, thud* of Matteo's heart and his breathing firing into rapid. Abby felt the tension in him and she knew that Matteo wanted to drop her and run and do what her father should have all those years ago.

For her sake he didn't.

But then, at the last moment, when he recalled Hunter's "I tend to get there first" line, Abby felt the rip of tension in him.

'Please don't,' Abby begged when she felt him move to run but then his arms came tighter around her.

'I won't.'

He wanted to though.

Matteo now could barely breathe.

Abby could feel him struggle to contain himself. Matteo even with a hangover in fierce heat did not break a sweat, yet he was swimming in adrenaline and his shirt was drenched and his breathing was coming fast and shallow.

'I might need to borrow that paper bag...' Matteo said.

Still he could make her smile.

And she waited for the questions to start but when her breathing was normal and she peered out from his chest, the only thing Matteo asked was if she wanted some water.

'Please.'

He went off to a vending machine and got her a drink and Abby drank it down thirstily, and Matteo was right; the panic had passed.

'Better?' Matteo asked.

'Much,' Abby said, though she was now incredibly embarrassed at what she had told him.

'So, where do you want to go now?' Matteo asked.

'Go?' It was the last thing she'd expected him to ask her but Matteo squatted down in front of her and looked right at her when, embarrassed by her revelations, she could barely now look at him.

'We're still celebrating your win.' Matteo was insistent. He looked briefly over to the team, who were all on their phones and buoyantly posing for the cameras and Kedah was with them. 'I'm guessing that you don't want to go out with that lot...'

'No.'

'But you won,' Matteo said. 'And you have every day since that bastard did what he did, and do you know what? You deserve to celebrate.'

'I do.'

'So, go and congratulate Pedro. Tell him it's covered tonight, whatever he wants.'

'Er, I don't know if you know what you're agreeing to.'

'You're talking to me.' Matteo smiled. 'I know what a wild night is. Seriously, with the bet I put on I'm even more loaded than usual. I'll get Kedah to go along with them. He runs wild but he's a good sort. He'll keep an eye.'

Matteo didn't, Abby thought, look at her like she had two heads; he just chatted away as if she hadn't just told him her darkest shame. 'You're sure?' she checked.

'Of course,' Matteo said. 'Kedah will cover it and then I'll see him right.'

He went to the vending machine again and bought a cola for himself and another water for her, and then Abby did what she properly wanted to do but hadn't had a chance to until now!

'Pedro!' She went over and gave him a hug.

'How good was that?' Pedro grinned. 'Hunter's spewing.'

'I know that he is. You were amazing, Pedro. I couldn't believe it when you took him. I still don't know how you did that.'

'I'll tell you in detail over dinner tonight,' Pedro said.

'Actually, I can't make dinner. I'm going to go out and chat up our sponsor,' Abby said. She saw a little flare of relief in her crew that she wasn't coming out with him, though they did their best to hide it.

'Oh, come on, Abby,' Pedro insisted but she shook her head.

Yes, they all got on, but it was a very male world and she saw the tiny smiles as they realised that they wouldn't have to behave as they always did around her.

And that thought brought a lump to her throat.

But these were nice tears that she was holding back.

They all *did* behave around her; she already knew that but she fully realised it then.

Abby's team really were amazing.

'Go and have the best night,' Abby told them. 'It's

all covered, whatever you want. Kedah will pick up the tab and Matteo will cover it.'

Pedro frowned. 'Are you sure?'

'Yes! Now go and have a brilliant night!' Abby said. 'God knows you deserve it but,' she warned, 'remember that we've got an official breakfast tomorrow.'

'Tell Matteo,' Pedro said, 'that I'll take him out in the car next time.'

'I shall.' She gave Pedro another hug and then she turned and went back to Matteo.

'Okay, where are we off to?' he asked.

'I don't know.'

'I do.' Matteo had just decided. 'First, though, we'll swing by my hotel and I'll get changed.'

'I need to get changed too.'

He looked down at her oily bottle-green overalls. 'Absolutely, you do!'

'Buy a dress here...' Matteo suggested as they pulled up at his hotel. 'There are plenty of boutiques for you to choose from.'

'No, I bought a dress ages ago and I promised that if we ever got on the podium...' Abby shook her head. 'I just never expected it to be tonight.'

She simply couldn't believe it.

Podium would have been brilliant—it would have shown that they were serious contenders—but to have come first was beyond her wildest dreams!

For others it was a nightmare—the bookies were panicking, the other teams were regrouping. Tonight, only the Boucher team was floating on cloud nine.

As they got out of his car Matteo was about to ask if she wanted to come up and have a drink while he changed but then he decided against it. Now her comment that first day, about their meeting being held in the restaurant rather than his hotel room, made sense.

God, he could kick himself now for the other night but instead he saw her to a seat and gave her a smile.

'I shan't be long.'

Abby sat in the lovely foyer as he went and changed and as she did she saw that she had about fifty missed calls, some from her father, and loads of texts offering congratulations. Where had they all been prior to this victory? Abby thought.

She turned her phone off and then she looked up as a man who had been there for her came out of the elevator. He was wearing black pants and a white shirt and dark tie but he was carrying the jacket to his suit, and he'd shaved.

For her.

And she remembered their kiss and her response and there were just too many feelings for Abby to explore right now, and so she chose to just do her best to enjoy the night.

Matteo had ditched his car and they were driven to her hotel and, instead of sitting in the car while she changed, he came into the foyer.

'My turn to wait,' he said.

Matteo sat down as she headed off to the elevators but he watched as Abby was called back by the concierge and signed for something and then, a few minutes later, she was handed a parcel and took the elevator up.

Abby stepped into her room .

She was dizzy both from elation at winning and her revelations about Hunter but it was the kiss that had taken place between her and Matteo that had her slightly breathless with recall.

Being kissed by Matteo had been amazing, showing her a side to herself she hadn't known existed.

Did it even matter, now that she'd told him the truth? That there had been no one before or after Hunter.

She thought about what he said, how Hunter didn't count, and she liked that. Even if it made her a twenty-seven-year-old virgin.

She took the dress out of her wardrobe and, given today's events, decided that the dress was too much.

Much too much.

It was seductive, provocative and sexy and it was everything Abby had hoped that she might one day be able to be.

Not yet though.

She was scared of her own sexuality, scared that if she dressed up tonight, then somehow Matteo might think she was leading him on.

To nowhere.

Oh, she was messed up, Abby knew.

She opened the package that she had signed for and her teeth ground together as a formal invitation from her father, inviting her to his fundraiser, fell out. It was written on a thick cream card but there was also attached to it a letter, or rather a note.

Abby.
As discussed.

No signature, no kisses, no *Love from Dad.* Just the reminder that if she wanted money to support her team, then it came with conditions attached.

She didn't need the money so badly now but her decision not to go was starting to waver. Seeing Matteo and Allegra together, trying to do the right thing by their grandfather, had served as a very poignant reminder as to how far Abby's own family had fallen apart, particularly since her mother had died.

Abby peeled back the paper to reveal a walnut box and she undid the tiny clasp and the lid sprung open. Her legs folded beneath her and she sat on the bed staring at her mum's necklace…

With the silver metal, white diamonds and the green of the emeralds, it was, like her mother had been, beautiful. And, Abby thought, holding it up so it caught the late-afternoon sun, it was possibly the most perfect accessory for her dress.

It was like a sign—not that she should attend her father's function; that decision she would make later—it just felt as if her mother had stopped by to tell her well done.

'Oh, Mum.'

She thought of Anette, her mother, and how her marriage had been such an unhappy one.

Her father was a cruel, egotistical man and her mother, with all her family and support in France, just hadn't found it within herself to leave. Anette had known that Hugo would have made her life hell if she did. So she had settled for a quieter version of hell—a marriage for the sake of the children.

Abby had loved her mother so very much.

She still did.

Had she been alive, Abby knew that what had happened with Hunter would have been handled differently. Oh, Anette had been weak where her father was concerned but not when it came to her girls.

Wear the dress, Abby.

She could almost hear her mother's voice.

Be who you are, not who others dictate that you be.

Abby *could* hear her mother's voice now.

She had been fifteen when her mother had died but now she remembered a long conversation they had had and her mother's advice.

It hadn't made sense; even in her darkest days, Abby hadn't been able to unravel her mother's words. Abby had tried to be herself and speak her mind and look where that had got her.

At twenty-seven those words made far better sense now.

Abby showered and then pinned up her hair and put on her make-up and with nervous hands pulled on some panties that were a touch too sensible for such an amazing dress but which were all that she had.

And then she slipped on the dress and the feel of cool silk on her skin had her face on fire. It was backless and so there was no bra that would work with it. She could see her nipples.

It wasn't slutty; it really was incredibly beautiful.

She wore the flat jewelled sandals that she had worn to Allegra's gala and they worked better with the dress than heels.

It didn't need heels; what it needed, Abby knew, taking the necklace from the box, was this.

The necklace hung as if it had been designed solely for this night.

It drew the attention from thick nipples and it made her eyes a deeper green. Abby was almost scared of her own reflection because she looked sexy and wanton and she did not want to tease the tiger.

Yet she trusted Matteo not to bite.

It was the most contrary feeling in the world, given all she had been through, and with only instinct to guide her, Abby listened to her own voice now.

Both she and the dress would celebrate tonight.

Matteo waited.

Oh, he waited for way more than half an hour this time.

He wondered if Abby was having trouble getting into a denim dress and Doc Martens but just as he smiled at that thought the elevators opened and a shining, shy beauty stepped out.

She was in a dress that was a bruised shade of silver, just one polish away from gleaming, and around her throat was the reason Matteo had first made contact.

Not now.

Oh, he watched her walk towards him—too nervous and shy to be sexy. She was utterly gorgeous—and how the hell did he tell her the truth?

Never had he been more grateful for a goldfish attention span when it suited him. Matteo just dismissed the Lost Mistresses from his mind and dealt with now.

'You look...' What? Often Matteo stopped himself from saying what he wanted to with Abby; he didn't tonight. 'You are the most beautiful woman I have ever seen.'

And he felt the most responsible that he ever had towards another.

This was her night.

It wasn't a restaurant like any other that Abby had ever been to.

White, candlelit tables were set on a private beach. It was an outdoor restaurant that combined fine dining with a sunset that fired as pink as her cheeks as they were shown to their seats.

'Champagne?' Matteo asked, and it was as if they were starting again.

Which they were.

He knew the truth now and, more importantly, Abby felt safe to let down her guard with him. She knew, Abby just knew, that she could strip naked and dance like a banshee and still he would see her safely home.

'That would be lovely.'

The champagne was poured and the first thing he did was raise a glass.

'To the Boucher team. Well done, you!'

They ate delectable seafood and their fingers met in the fragrant bowls and they flirted a little but more than that they talked and they celebrated her win.

'Pedro's happy,' Matteo said.

'For now.' Abby nodded. 'I've been watching him for years, since he was about sixteen. I know he's good and that he's thrilled with the win but he's not going to hang around for long and I can't blame him for that.'

'Is *that* why it has to be this year that you win the Henley Cup?'

That being Hunter.

Abby hesitated and then nodded.

'He retires this year. I want my revenge,' she admitted. 'I know it's supposed to be healthier to forgive…'

Matteo snorted, which told her what he thought of that!

'You're going to do it,' he said. 'But if not this year, there's still next. Don't make your life about him.'

'I know.'

'Concentrate on keeping Pedro sweet,' Matteo said. 'Spoil him. You've got winnings now.'

'He placed fifth here last year,' Abby said. 'It was our first race and he should have been way back but, like today, something happened. He's a genius and now everyone really knows it.' She told Matteo something. 'The next night, after he placed fifth, he took me out for dinner. He was just twenty then and I'm his manager and yet he got the bill and I knew that I was being served notice. He told me that he'd already been approached by the Lachance team. We came to a deal and I asked for this year, for the Henley Cup.'

'Things are different now,' Matteo said. 'He's part of a winning team and it *is* a team—a progressive one. The Lachance mob are sticking to the same old formulas. Remind him of that.'

'I shall,' Abby agreed. 'Pedro wants to take you for a spin when we get to Milan.'

'No, thank you,' Matteo said, and Abby raised her eyes in surprise. She had thought, given his daredevil nature, that he would jump at the chance, but he'd shaken his head at the offer.

'Thanks for today.' Abby addressed what she had to, glad that it was getting darker and so he hopefully couldn't see that her face was on fire.

'For what?'

'I've never had a panic attack before, not a full-blown one. I thought I was going to die.'

'I told you that you wouldn't.'

'You said that your sister got them?'

Matteo nodded but said no more.

'I didn't expect to react like that. I've seen him around before, of course.'

Matteo didn't like that and he frowned.

'We're on tour at the same time,' Abby pointed out. 'I always make sure that we're in separate hotels. I only really see him trackside and usually I'm fine. Well, not fine exactly but I've never had that happen to me.'

'He was angry today,' Matteo said. 'Even if he was trying to hide it.'

'Yes.'

'And I would expect that brought some stuff up for you.'

'I guess,' Abby said. 'I hate how he's messed me up.'

'Messed up?' Matteo checked. 'Hardly! Your team just won—you're coming into your own.'

'You know what I mean.' She had said way more than she had wanted to today but she *had* said it—there had been no one since Hunter.

'It's just a matter of time,' Matteo said.

'It's been nine years!'

He actually grinned. 'How the hell do you sleep?' he asked. 'I need a drink or sex, preferably both.' He thought for a moment. 'You're not frigid. Had there not been one hundred thousand people watching on, I could have had you this afternoon.'

'Exceptional circumstances!' Abby said.

He just spoke about it in such a matter-of-fact way that it made the world a bit nicer but she shook her head at the impossibility. 'He seriously messed with my head.'

'We're all messed up, Abby.'

'You're not.'

'Of course I am. My whole family are.'

'Because your parents died?' Abby asked.

'Because of how they lived.'

It was Abby who didn't know what to say now.

Matteo never opened up to anyone. He could talk for hours and still reveal little about himself but with all she had told him today, well, it seemed wrong to hold back. He looked at her, so stunning on the outside and so churned up within, and it felt unfair to let her think that the polished, carefree man who sat before her didn't have dark memories of his own.

'Do you know why I said no to Pedro taking me for a spin?'

She shook her head.

'Because the thought of having someone drive me around at high speed makes me ill.'

'But riding a thoroughbred racehorse doesn't?' Abby frowned.

'When I was five my father woke me up in the

middle of the night. Now, when I look back, he was high on cocaine but I didn't know about drugs then. I just knew there were times we avoided him and that this was one of those times. He'd won a car.' Matteo sat there for a moment and remembered his bewilderment at being woken up. 'We had loads of cars, but no, he had to show me this one. He took me into the garage and I remember that the car was silver. He told me how fast it went and just all this stuff and then he told me to climb in. I did...' He looked at Abby, and Matteo was probably more confused in hindsight than he had been at the time. 'Do you know, he didn't even check if I was belted in? He just revved that engine and took off.'

'To where?' Abby asked.

'Everywhere,' Matteo said. 'It was the longest night of my life, changing lanes, swerving, all the lights blurring. I wet myself,' Matteo admitted. 'He just kept going faster. He was laughing and shouting. I swear I knew we were going to die that night but somehow we made it home. A few weeks later there was a huge fight and my father got loaded. My mother got in the car, apparently to sort things out once and for all. They say the car skidded out of control but I always wonder...'

'If she was as scared as you had been?'

'Yep,' Matteo said. 'She'd got clean by then, well, apart from spending...' He saw her slight frown. 'Believe me, I almost wish she hadn't though. I can't stand the thought that she might have been as sober and as scared as I was that night.'

'What do your brothers and sisters say?'

'There are some things that you just don't discuss. We talk about other things, but the past is there—we all know it. I'm sure they have their own memories and issues. I've never told anyone about that night.' He gave her a wry smile. 'So, no—tell Pedro thanks but no thanks. I shan't be taking him up on his offer.'

He tipped the last of the champagne into her glass.

'Enough of the sad stuff,' he said. 'We're supposed to be celebrating.'

They danced on the beach, a lovely long, slow dance, and Abby was celebrating not just the win, nor that she was out in her sexy silver dress and necklace, drinking champagne and relaxed, but turned on in his arms. But that this emotionally elusive man had told her something about himself.

Something that not even his family knew.

It was, without doubt, for Abby, the perfect end to the perfect day.

Matteo thought it less than perfect. Not the day, nor the night—more what he had found out. What had happened to Abby was criminal, not just the event but the effect that it had had on her.

For the first time that he could remember he wanted to step up, but that would mean offering more than he had sworn to ever do.

He remembered their kiss and could feel the attraction but the cruellest thing in the world would be to let her think he was capable of even a short-term relationship. And so, when the music ended Matteo did as promised.

He took her safely home.

CHAPTER SIX

ABBY WOKE AND stretched and looked over to her lovely silver dress that was draped over the chair and she was more mixed up than ever.

Matteo confused her almost as much she confused herself.

She wanted him.

Oh, my, she wanted him, and last night had been perfect.

Absolutely perfect except for one thing.

Unlike the sensual kiss they had shared after the win, at the end of last night, when he'd taken her back to the hotel, Matteo had briefly kissed her on the cheek like he was saying goodbye to some elderly moustached aunt.

Maybe all that she'd told him had been a bit too much.

And, Abby conceded, Matteo was way too much to be cutting her teeth on. He didn't do relationships—he had made that blatantly clear—and Abby really was the last person to consider a casual relationship.

Except she was.

She was lying in bed, in pyjamas, and wondering what it would be like to have sex with Matteo.

In fact, since the first night they'd met she'd often found herself lying in bed wondering the very same.

Instead of dwelling on that lovely thought, when there was a knock at the door she pulled back the covers and answered it.

It wasn't breakfast, just the coffee she had ordered, given that they had an official breakfast starting in less than an hour.

She wondered how the team would shape up this morning.

Abby got dressed. There were several issues being a woman in a very male world and the Boucher corporate wear was one of them.

Bottle-green men's trousers.

Yum.

A bottle-green shirt and a black belt and lovely flat black shoes.

She headed down to the restaurant and there, looking very seedy but dressed in bottle-green, were her team.

'How was last night?' Abby asked.

'Kedah's a bad influence,' Pedro said. 'I can see pink elephants.'

'Just keep smiling,' Abby said.

'Kedah wants to sponsor us too!' Pedro told her.

Breakfast was long and there were an awful lot

of photos and after that there were even more inter-
views for poor Pedro.

'How's Pedro doing?' Abby jumped at the sound
of Matteo's voice.

'Very well,' she said. 'I wasn't expecting to see
you this morning.'

'We'll talk in a moment,' Matteo said. 'I just want
to catch up with Pedro.' He went over and whatever
he had to say to Pedro took ages and then finally he
came over to her.

'Can we go somewhere?' Matteo asked and Abby
nodded; he had his business face on and looked tired.

They found a table and she ordered tea and Matteo did the same.

'You don't look like you've slept,' she commented.

'I haven't,' Matteo admitted. 'And neither has my
lawyer.'

Abby frowned.

'I'm in,' Matteo said.

'Officially?'

'Yes.' He handed her a very thick contract. 'In a
nutshell, I'll be your sponsor for the next eighteen
months. You can back out at any time. I can't. Take
your time to go through it though.'

She skimmed the first couple of pages and saw the
figures he was talking and, no, she couldn't imagine backing out.

'What do you get out of it?' Abby asked.

'The Di Sione name on your car and Pedro, as

well as your disgusting shirt…' He looked at her attire. 'Can we add a clause about your clothes? You're wearing the same as the men.'

'We can!' Abby smiled. 'What else?'

'That's pretty much it. Abby, I love the racing world. I can see why you're completely hooked.'

'It's not always this good,' she warned. 'In fact, it's never been this good till now and it might not be again.'

'I get that,' Matteo said. 'I've just spoken to Pedro and when we're both in New York I'm taking him shopping for a car. I'll deal with his ego,' he said and Abby let out a breath of relief. 'You can concentrate on the cars.'

It felt too good to be true and she waited for Matteo to reveal the catch as he carried on speaking. 'Now, go through the contract and flag any concerns that you have but when you read it, know that I'm in, no matter what happens between us.'

Abby looked up from the contract she was reading.

It had been business but now he had sideswiped her.

'Us?'

'Do I have to spell it out?'

'I think so.'

'I don't do relationships,' Matteo said. 'I never have and I never will but I think we both know we're heading for bed.'

'I don't know that,' Abby flustered.

'Of course you do.' Matteo stated it as fact. 'And, as I said the day we met, I am very patient. So, don't stress about cup-winning performances on that front either. We'll take it slow, get you enjoying it. Just know that when we're miserable exes, and loathe each other, I'll still be here for the team.'

He meant it.

For the best part of the night and well into the morning he had been speaking with his lawyer and playing email ping-pong with him.

In between all of that though, he had been thinking about Abby.

A future for the two of them was impossible but a future for Abby he could envisage, and he knew that much he could help her with.

'Matteo…'

'I have to go,' he said. 'I'm heading back to New York. I've got a big meeting tomorrow. I know no one thinks I do anything but I do work…'

He'd just offered her millions in sponsorship and a few sex lessons to boot and now he was dashing off.

'Get yourself on the pill,' he said. 'I'll do all the health checks.'

'Health checks?'

'They're not really necessary,' Matteo said. 'I always wear a condom but I shan't with you.' He gave her a smile that had her thighs squeeze together at the top. 'We don't want a break in proceedings,' Matteo said and in the most awkward of subjects still he made her smile. 'No pit stops to change the rubber. We'll just keep the momentum going.'

Pedro came over then. 'Are you okay, Abby?' He checked, no doubt, because her face was on fire.

'I'm fine.'

'Well,' Matteo said in his best business voice. 'I've given you a lot to think about, Abby. I'll see you in Milan.'

It was a month away!

'As I said,' Matteo carried on. 'I shan't be breathing down your neck.'

He shook her hand, shook Pedro's and then he was gone.

'Matteo said I could have his jet at my disposal for a week if I bring in the Henley Cup,' Pedro said. 'He's my man crush.'

Abby shot Pedro a look. 'Hands off,' she said and they both laughed.

It was the first time she'd laughed with a friend about something so basic and nice.

CHAPTER SEVEN

MATTEO DID EXACTLY as he had said he would and was completely hands off.

Abby was the recipient of several emails from some virtual assistant with flight itineraries and suchlike.

The contract was signed and countersigned.

Sheikh Kedah wanted to sponsor them too, but of all the amazing things that were happening, the one that had Abby reeling the most was that she was ankles in stirrups and having a pelvic exam and that she left the clinic with six shiny packets of contraceptive pills.

She still didn't know what would happen between them.

And that wasn't Abby being coy or naive. She was seriously crazy about Matteo but she was also seriously crazy about her work. Yes, the contract might be watertight but sniping at her sponsor she didn't need.

And Abby *would* snipe.

Oh, the giddy high of being with Matteo would be wonderful, Abby knew, but she'd been clearly warned that it would only be temporary.

Abby *was* a sore loser; it was the reason she'd got as far as she had in the racing world.

Losing Matteo, or rather the flirting and friendship and fun of them…well, it was something she treasured and Abby wasn't completely sure she wanted to mess with what they had.

And he was reckless.

The more she knew him, the more she read about him, the more debauched Matteo's lifestyle appeared.

Still, it was bliss to know that the flights were covered, and with that weight off her mind the race ahead had never had greater attention.

Abby even found the time for coffee with her friend Bella one morning, while Matteo took Pedro out for that shopping spree. Given that Bella was an engineer on the Carter team they had a *very* strict no-inside-info rule, but it was lovely to catch up.

'Are you still walking on air after Dubai?' Bella grinned.

'I think we're all just trying to get our head in the game for Milan, but yes,' Abby admitted. 'It still feels brilliant.'

'And how on earth did you land a Di Sione as a sponsor?' Bella couldn't help but pry. 'I'm not sharing details but you must surely know that everyone is put out? Who wouldn't want a Di Sione sponsor? Even one as wild as Matteo.'

Abby smiled. 'Just luck. I think he likes taking risks and, given our new status, we're the biggest risk of them all.'

'I think he's the risk rather than you,' Bella said and rolled her eyes. 'Front page again.'

Abby frowned and Bella groaned. 'Sorry, I thought you would have already seen the news. It's everywhere,' Bella said and handed Abby her phone.

There was Matteo, staring at the camera, but instead of his regular suit or slightly bleary-eyed look as he came out of a casino, this image told her that he came in just under the six-foot-three line.

It was a mug shot.

Abby briefly scanned the article and found out that Matteo had been arrested last night after a fight in a very exclusive restaurant broke out and management had had no choice but to call the police.

Patrons were shocked and distressed.

'That's Matteo.' Abby shrugged and handed back the phone, and she managed a wry smile and a roll of her eyes while on the inside her heart sunk.

He was supposed to be picking up Pedro now and her young driver had been looking forward to the day with Matteo so much.

It wasn't just that he had let down Pedro that upset her. Matteo created chaos; a night in wasn't enough for him, nor a nice meal by the looks of things. It had to be drama; it had to end on a dangerous high.

That was the man she was considering sleeping with!

Well, not any more.

Abby truly didn't know what to say. She could hardly tell Bella how crazy she was about him, nor how disappointed she was in him too.

Instead she called Pedro but, unable to get hold of him, she gave up and Abby did her best to forget about Matteo and whatever the latest trouble he found himself in. They chatted about some of the other teams, leaving their own out, and Bella also told her that she was serious about someone.

'In the racing world?' Abby asked.

'Oh, no!' Bella shook her head. 'I had to change the battery in his car.' She laughed. 'He hasn't a clue and that suits me fine. I'm keeping romance well away from work—I've had my fingers burnt way too many times in the past.'

It would serve her well to remember that, Abby thought as she drove home.

Tomorrow they flew to Milan. Once there, the car, which had been pulled apart and shipped after the Dubai race, would be meticulously put back together again and training would begin in earnest—fine-tuning the car and ensuring it was perfect for the practice race, and then she would make the final modifications for the race itself.

Now though, there was one brief night to relax. Not that she could.

Damn you, Matteo, Abby thought as she turned on the news and sure enough the first thing she saw was his mug shot.

Abby switched it off and, when the doorbell rang, she hauled herself from the sofa and there at the door stood Pedro.

A very different-looking Pedro.

His hair had been cropped and he was wearing a sharp suit and, judging by the set of keys he was waving, he was the new owner of a car fit for a soon-to-be racing legend.

'Matteo made it to take you out?' Abby put her own anger aside and smiled as she let Pedro in. 'How was it?'

'It was brilliant.'

'I tried to call you,' Abby said.

'I left my phone at Bernadette's. I'm just on my way there now.'

'So what happened with Matteo?' Abby couldn't stop herself from asking. 'I saw on the news that he'd been arrested…'

'And released without charge.' Pedro shrugged as he walked into her lounge. 'Some guy was arguing with his wife and got heavy. Matteo stepped in and the guy took his mood out on him. Hey, Abby…' Pedro said to his very distracted manager, who was blowing out a guilty breath at her own presumption.

'I wanted to ask you something—can Bernadette come to Milan?'

Abby guessed Matteo had suggested that Pedro ask her.

Pedro had wanted to bring Bernadette last time but things had been so incredibly tight that there had been no room for wives and girlfriends.

Things were different now.

'Sure.' Abby nodded.

She wanted Pedro to linger, to tell her all about his day, or rather anything else Matteo had even loosely mentioned, but he was soon heading off to show Bernadette his new clothes and car and to tell her the news. Abby spent the rest of the night wondering if Matteo would call.

He didn't.

And so, by the time the team were due to fly to Milan, Abby was in a state of high anticipation at seeing him.

She felt a bit like a schoolmistress at an all-male school as they boarded the Di Sione jet. Everyone was in high spirits, everyone except Abby, because there was no sign of Matteo.

Abby sat in a plush leather seat and rolled her eyes as Pedro looked around the jet.

'Who gets the suite?'

'You do!' The attendant smiled.

It was then, Abby knew, Matteo wasn't joining them.

* * *

Milan she glimpsed from the inside of a luxurious coach that took them from the airport to the hotel.

Abby knew the hotel the Lachance team stayed at and she had chosen another one, as she always did, which gave her one less thing to worry about.

Everyone was checked in but Abby lingered till they had all headed off to their rooms and then she asked the receptionist if there were any messages for her.

There weren't.

'Is Matteo Di Sione here yet?' Abby made herself ask.

'No.'

'Do you know when he's arriving?'

'We can't give out that sort of information.'

'I'm a colleague,' Abby attempted but she was no match for the tight security around the Di Sione name. 'A close colleague.'

'Then ask him.' The receptionist's smile did not waver. 'Is there anything else that I can help you with?'

It was a busy week with little waking time to dwell on Matteo and when and if he would arrive.

Despite their amazing win, Abby did know it was unlikely to be replicated.

Pedro had raced the Dubai course but never Milan and, though they went over and over it and watched endless recordings of previous races, she could feel Pedro's tension.

'I shouldn't have brought Bernadette,' he admitted to Abby before he put on his helmet for the practice run. 'She's going to see me place last.'

'Don't think about that,' Abby said.

'I just got a text from Matteo, wishing me luck...'

It was more than she'd had.

'I've a feeling I shan't be getting his jet for a week.'

'Listen,' Abby said to Pedro. 'You won last month. Nothing can take that away.'

'Yeah, but I've got a whole lot more to prove now. Hunter reckons it was a fluke—he was talking in Reception loud enough for me to hear.'

Abby took a steadying breath. Apparently there had been a problem with the Lachance team's hotel security and yesterday they had moved to the one Abby's team were staying at.

Still, her own nervousness as to that wasn't the issue now.

'Don't listen to anything Hunter says.' Abby spoke firmly. 'Don't even look at him. Just give him the finger in your head any time you pass him. Maybe not today, but any time in your career that you pass him, then that's what you'll do.'

And so, too, would she.

The practice run didn't go particularly well and Abby spent ages trying to soothe Pedro, who was seriously rattled, but finally at six he headed back to the hotel for an early dinner and then bed. Abby worked till late making modifications to the car.

By the time she got back to the hotel Abby was hungry, tired and certainly not looking the way she would want Matteo to see her, but there he was checking in at Reception.

Abby kept walking.

A month of no contact and she didn't know where they were at and so she made her way to the elevator and pressed the button and stood.

'Don't you say hello?' Matteo asked and she turned and smiled as he came and stood beside her.

'I didn't know if you'd just wanted to go up to your suite and crash,' Abby admitted.

'I do.' Matteo yawned. It had been a very long day. 'So, how's the race preparation going?' he asked as their elevator arrived and they stepped in.

'It hasn't been the best day.' Abby sighed. 'Pedro's convinced that he's peaked too soon, though he seems a bit calmer now.'

'Yes, I saw the press conference,' Matteo said. 'He looked like he was about to throw up. What have you been doing?'

'I've been working on the car.' The elevator stopped at her floor. 'Do you want to get dinner?' Abby suggested.

'I'm just going to get room service,' Matteo said. 'Do you want to come up…?' He stopped. 'Sorry,

that was thoughtless of me.' It had just seemed a
natural solution—he was tired and hungry and he
guessed, given the late hour, that Abby felt the same.
He just didn't want the bother of going down to the
restaurant.

He thought she'd be offended but Abby just smiled
at his discomfort.

'Matteo, it's fine,' she said. 'Room service sounds
great. I'm starving.'

It was actually the nicest thing that he could have
said to her, Abby thought—part of the difficulty of
revealing such sensitive secrets was the aftermath.

She had been worried that he might look at her
differently or think of her in different ways, but
clearly it wasn't at the top of his mind and that suited
Abby.

They went straight up to his floor and to his suite
and everything was better in Matteo's world. Abby
had thought she'd ordered the best suite for Pedro but
clearly there were others tucked away for the likes
of the Di Siones.

It was huge, more like a stately home than a hotel
suite. The shutters were open to a stunning view of
Milan at night but Matteo went straight over and
closed them. 'I'm sick of views,' he said.

Matteo's cases had already been brought up and
the butler was putting his stuff away but stopped
what he was doing and asked if he could get Matteo a drink.

'Please.' Matteo nodded.

Unlike the bar fridge in Abby's room, here there was a crystal decanter, presumably filled with Matteo's preferred cognac, but Abby shook her head when offered one. 'I'd love a cola.'

'And me,' Matteo said, and before too long they had been served their drinks and were alone, Abby with a lovely iced cola, Matteo with both of his favourite brews. He drained the cola and then took the cognac more slowly as he asked about the practice run.

'I have to say I'm not expecting a repeat of Dubai.'

'Pedro knew that track,' Matteo said and Abby gave a relieved nod, glad that he understood.

'I am worried though. Now that we've had a win there's so much expectation…'

'Not from me,' Matteo said. 'I just called Pedro before and said he's got the jet for a week whatever happens on Sunday. I suggested that he tell Bernadette *after* the race, wherever he places.'

Matteo took off his jacket and kicked off his shoes.

'You look tired,' Abby commented.

'I am. It's been one hell of a week.' Matteo yawned. 'Family stuff.'

'As well as getting arrested. How was lockup?'

'Same old.' Matteo shrugged.

He didn't want to think about that night. Not the

arrest, but the fight that he'd been privy to as he'd gone to the restroom.

Would he have turned away, if Abby hadn't told him what had happened to her?

No.

He might have called management or…

Matteo didn't know. All he did know was that he had seen red and pulled an angry man off his partner and told him to take his temper out on someone who stood a chance.

The bastard had taken him up on the offer.

Still it wasn't just the other night and his family that were on Matteo's mind though—even with an arrest and many nights out it had been a very long month.

A very tame month.

On many occasions he had wanted to pick up the phone and call Abby or step on a plane. He was walking a very fine line because sex was the easy part for Matteo.

Business he had taken care of through his lawyer and the contract was watertight.

It was the feelings he didn't know how to handle. It was Abby he couldn't get off his mind, Abby who he wanted to spend time with. Matteo knew his own reputation though, and he didn't want to give mixed messages—such as how much he'd missed her, how she stayed on his mind.

Instead he stood up and flicked through the restaurant menu but looked up when Abby, who was wandering around the suite, caught sight of her reflection in a mirror and let out a little yelp—her face was streaked in oil.

'I think I should go have a bath and get changed before dinner,' Abby said.

'Have a bath here…' Matteo said and then grimaced. God, every time he said something it came out wrong. 'I meant…'

'I know,' Abby said. 'And I know, given all I've told you, that being in your hotel room should be awkward, but honestly, Matteo—' she gave a tight shrug, unsure just how to voice it '—it isn't.'

She just didn't feel nervous around him. It was during times apart that she did.

'Matteo?' Abby checked because he really was behaving oddly. 'Is everything okay?'

'No,' he admitted and came over to her. 'This is how I wanted to say hello.' He put his arms around her and it was the nicest place to be and he kissed her, a slow gentle kiss, the type that chased the day away. 'I've missed you.'

'You could have called.'

'I thought you said that you wanted a hands-off sponsor.'

He was very hands on now—they were resting on her waist and she could feel the weight of them and the heat of his palms.

'You don't just have to call about the team.'

'I know that,' Matteo said, 'but then I'm not really big on the "how was your day" type of phone call.' He was as honest as he could be about something he didn't really understand, because he'd never really felt the need to be in touch with another, for no reason other than to be in touch. 'And then if I call one week and then don't the next…' He gave a tense shrug. 'I don't do all that.'

And therein was the difference, Abby thought. Matteo was struggling to commit to a call a week! Their heads were in completely different spaces. The way Abby felt, a call an hour would barely do.

'You've got oil on your face now,' Abby said and they peeled apart enough to see the mess she had made of his shirt.

'Have a bath,' he said, because hell, he wasn't letting that bastard change how he spoke to her or the things that he did. 'Either go down and have one, or have one here, but I'm wrecked and I'm having dinner in bed, or rather on top of it, and you're not getting on covered in oil.'

'Didn't you sleep on the plane?'

'No,' Matteo said. 'I had some work to catch up on.'

He let her go and picked up the menu and read through it.

'Sometimes all you need is a good steak,' Matteo said.

'Sounds great,' Abby said. 'I'll have mine well done.'

'Philistine.'

He rang and ordered as Abby headed off to the bathroom and, yes, it was so nice to peel off filthy clothes and step into a deep, fragrant bath and know that dinner was on the way and that Matteo was here.

Abby lay there, eyes closed, just enjoying the sensation of the water and the low sound of Matteo chatting on the phone on the other side of the door.

Then she heard a knock on the door to his suite and from the sound of it dinner had arrived. Abby hauled herself out of the bath.

It had done its magic.

She was clean and scented and all the tension of the day seemed to have gone, Abby thought as she pulled on a robe and opened up one of the hotel combs and ran it through her hair.

She came out of the bathroom and saw that he wasn't in the lounge but it didn't take long to find him. There was Matteo lying on the top of the bed with a large silver trolley by its side and he'd taken his shirt off.

'It had oil on it,' Matteo said as she tried not to look at his naked top half. 'And,' he added, 'I have to sleep in this bed tonight—you don't.'

'I'm very used to the smell of oil,' Abby said and, as he'd more or less told her that it would be closing time in the Di Sione suite soon, she relaxed. Dinner smelled amazing and she handed him his rare steak and she couldn't help but look at his chest. He was slender but muscular and her eyes were drawn to his ribcage and she saw an old yellowing bruise there, she presumed from the fight the other night.

God, that body took a battering.

'How's the shoulder?' Abby asked.

'I have near-full range of movement,' Matteo said.

Even that sounded suggestive as she took her plate to the other side of the bed and climbed on.

'I love having dinner in bed,' Matteo said, showering his steak in pepper.

'I don't think I've ever had it.' Abby thought for a moment. 'Well, unless I've been sick.'

'You know that full feeling when you just want to lie down?' he asked. 'I was going to open a restaurant once, just beds. Dante and Dario talked me out of it.'

'Your brothers?' Abby checked.

'They're far more savvy than me. They started Libertine?'

'The app for the wealthy?' Abby had heard of it. His family really was everywhere!

'Yes, it provides anything for anyone, just so long as you can afford it. Anyway, I accepted their advice that my bedside restaurant chain wasn't the best idea, though I still think it could work.'

'Nobody would ever leave.' Abby smiled.

She didn't want to leave.

'What about…' Matteo had been about to ask about her sister but he kept having to remind himself of what Abby had told him and what her father had. 'What about you?' he asked instead. 'Any brothers or sisters?'

'An older sister,' Abby said. 'Annabel. We've never really got on.'

'Because?'

'Because I make things complicated apparently. She's married to my father.' Abby rolled her eyes. 'Well, not my father exactly but…'

'I get the picture.'

'She's pregnant,' Abby said. 'With her first. At the end of October I'll be an aunt and I haven't seen my sister in years.'

'At all?'

Abby shook her head. 'We talk on the phone at Christmas and things but I haven't been home for a long time.'

'Years?'

She nodded but didn't elaborate.

Abby didn't want to spoil this night with people who weren't them.

It was just so nice to eat and then to lie there side by side and to talk.

And because it was so nice and they were both so relaxed Matteo tried to tell her some of what was on his mind.

The Origins of Them, as he called it.

'Hey, you know your necklace…'

'It's not actually mine,' Abby said. 'It's my father's.'

'Yes, but…' He hesitated for a beat too long and Abby continued speaking.

'My mother left it to him. He's got a big do in July and has told me that he wants me there, looking presentable and wearing the necklace.'

Matteo swallowed.

'I'm not going to go though.'

He breathed out a sigh of relief. 'How come?'

'We don't really talk. Well, not since…' She didn't want to discuss it again and so she changed the subject a little. 'There's a huge party in LA on the same night. Anyone who placed in the Henley Cup will be there and so now I've got a legitimate reason not to go to my father's function.' She looked at him. 'You should come.'

'Why?'

'You're our sponsor…'

'And?'

The relief that she wasn't going to her father's function, just the little rush of being let off the hook, had Matteo stop worrying about the problems that beset them, and he moved a little closer and started playing with the tie to her robe.

Yes, Matteo decided, he'd tell her about her father and the necklace but at a better time.

After the race, maybe?

'Have you thought about what I said about us two?'

'I have.' Abby answered him as casually as she could—as if she hadn't spent way too many hours poring over his words. Now was the time to say no, that it was perhaps the most stupid of ideas, yet, side-on facing each other, his fingers found the swell of her nipple, even through the thick robe, and he stroked it, just not enough for Abby.

'And?' Matteo asked.

'I don't know,' Abby admitted.

'Better than a no,' Matteo said. 'At least it's something to work on.'

Which he was. She could feel his fingers at the very tip of her breast but as his lips found hers, Matteo's hand flattened and the pressure of his warm palm was divine. It was a different kiss to the one they'd shared earlier; this was a sexy kiss and his naked torso she now explored beneath her hands and he let her. Odd that at twenty-seven it was more than she'd done with a man. His leg came over hers and then Matteo's fingers were at the tie of her robe, but he held back from peeling it open.

Abby wanted him to.

God, she loathed that she tied double knots.

His lips moved from her mouth and to her neck and Abby's hands drifted down, feeling his toned stomach right to the edge of his belt, and she wanted so much to move her hand farther down but resisted.

Matteo had endless patience but that didn't make

him blind to need and if she so much as moved to halt him, then he would, but instead they just carried on kissing as he made light work of her robe.

Now he peeled it open and so their chests were naked and touching, just enough to ensure it was not enough.

'Don't rush me,' Abby said, which was contrary to how she felt.

'I'm kicking you out in five minutes,' Matteo said and then he took her hand and placed it where she wanted it to be. His tongue caressed hers and she explored him through the fabric, hard and straining, and she ached to set him free but opened her eyes and met his gaze.

Oh, she wanted.

But she wanted more too.

More than Matteo would ever give.

'I don't want to lead you on,' Abby said, 'if I don't…'

'You can lead me on any time.'

'I'm going to go down,' Abby said, her hand still on him and his smile made her smile. 'I meant to my room.'

'I know,' Matteo said. 'A guy can dream.'

He made her feel sexy, so much so that she wanted to do just what the suggestive air called.

He could actually feel her reluctance as Abby got off the bed and it felt like a win to Matteo. He'd never really got the saying "it's worth the wait." Matteo waited for no one, impulse never lasted that long and he went with them at whim.

She would be worth the wait though.

As Abby went into the en suite to retrieve her clothes Matteo called her back.

'You can't put those back on.'

'Well, I'm not going down in my robe.'

'Send the butler to get you a change of clothes, then,' Matteo said and went to reach for the phone but Abby halted him.

'No, he'll think…'

'Who *cares* what he thinks?'

'I care.'

'God, you're a prude,' Matteo said but not nastily. 'I'll go and get something for you to wear.' He really was nice like that, Abby thought as he got out of bed and put on a fresh shirt. 'I can have a little rummage through your underwear drawer while I'm there!'

She handed over her room card and Matteo headed out to the elevators.

He wanted her to stay, yet he didn't want to push, Matteo thought as he pressed the button for the tenth floor.

And then, as the elevator stopped at the eighteenth floor and Hunter stepped in, Matteo changed his mind.

He wanted Abby in his room and the thought that she might be here, in this elevator dressed in her robe and alone with Hunter right now, had Matteo holding his breath.

He leaned back on the brass rail of the elevator as Hunter stared ahead and Matteo's eyes never left his face.

Yes, Hunter knew who he was, Matteo knew, because he could see a muscle flickering in his cheek and the tension was near boiling point.

He could take him here now, Matteo thought.

Wipe him out of any chance of racing tomorrow, but Abby would hate that, he knew.

She wanted to beat him herself, in her own way.

The elevator stopped at the tenth floor, only Matteo didn't get out; he didn't want Hunter to even have a hint that this was Abby's floor.

The doors closed again and it was then that Hunter spoke.

'Problem?' Hunter asked because Matteo's stare could blister paint.

'Just the smell,' Matteo answered and then, as the elevator opened, when Matteo knew he should just let Hunter go, instead he offered a very choice word.

Hunter stiffened but he didn't turn around; instead he carried on walking but there was a dangerous, unchecked energy between them and Matteo could feel his heart thumping as he pressed floors five through to twelve and the elevator started moving again.

Matteo got to Abby's room.

The turn-down service had been and there was a

chocolate on her pillow and it was all calm but his heart still thumped in his chest and so he poured a glass of water and took a drink.

Abby had told him that they always stayed at different hotels.

He closed his eyes and tried to tell himself to calm down. They were in the same profession, Matteo said to himself. Of course their paths would cross.

The self-talk didn't reassure.

Matteo went to the wardrobe and pulled out a top and a skirt and then he went to her underwear drawer. Next he went over to the bed and wrote a silly note and left it on her pillow, then back up to his suite he went.

One look at his face and Abby knew something was wrong.

'Here.' He handed her her clothes; he was about to suggest that she get changed and then he would walk her down, or maybe that it wasn't such a good idea for her to be staying at this hotel and that they could switch, but the long sentence sort of shrunk into three words.

'Stay here tonight.'

'Matteo?'

'Hunter's here.'

'There was a problem with security and so they…'

'No, no…' Matteo wasn't buying it for a moment. 'Did you really think he was just going to let you take him down without a fight, Abby? Did you think, when you were hatching your master plan, that Hunter was just going to sit back and let you beat him?'

'It's not going to happen again,' Abby said.

'I'm not saying that it is,' Matteo said. 'But you've stirred up a hornet's nest and he's angry.'

'Did you say anything?' Abby demanded.

'He knows that I know what happened.'

'What did you say to him?' Abby shouted. 'Matteo, you didn't do...'

'I didn't do anything,' he snapped. 'He already thought I knew at the press conference. I just let him know tonight that I did. Abby, that guy swaggers around... I swear that he's going to do whatever it takes to mess with your head.'

'He's already messed with Pedro's,' she admitted.

Matteo was right, Abby realised—it was no accident that Hunter was here.

'Stay,' Matteo said. 'I'm not going to try anything.' And then he shouted, nicely if that was possible, 'I just want you in my bed with me!'

'Matteo, you're not always going to be around,' Abby pointed out.

But he was the master of instant fixes. 'Let's just get through tonight.'

Matteo was shaken, in a way that he never had been about another.

Sex really was the last thing on his mind tonight.

It wasn't anything to do with that.

In fact, for Matteo, it was more concerning than that, because when he stripped off and got into bed, he just needed her skin beside his.

Abby stood there as Matteo stripped off.

Completely.

She guessed it wouldn't enter his head to get into bed any other way.

She could ask for pillows between them, or get into bed, her robe tied and her reluctance evident, only she wasn't reluctant.

It was her feelings for Matteo that scared her.

Not him.

She took off her robe and got in beside him and he switched off the light and just rolled into her.

He kissed her shoulder, the back of her hair and he ran a hand the length of her thigh and to her waist and then the *thump, thump* of his heart slowed and Abby lay there, listening to him sleeping with his hand resting on her stomach.

Abby slowly acclimatised to the feeling of sharing a bed with someone. She kept waiting for his hand to move, or for Matteo to change his mind about not trying anything. But Matteo was sleeping the sleep of the dead and so she found out what it was like to be held naked through the night with no expectation.

It was possibly the nicest gift of all and in that moment her world was the nicest place.

In the dark, next to him.

CHAPTER EIGHT

AT FIRST ABBY thought that she had jolted awake but then realised that the movement had come from Matteo.

He was still asleep but Matteo just had the familiar sensation of falling.

Only it wasn't him falling from a tree this time.

He was standing at the door to an elevator and watching the carriage drop down with Hunter and Abby in it and grabbing out for the cable and missing.

Yes, he jolted but then in that same instant felt her warm next to him and knew it was a dream and straight back into deep sleep he went.

Abby lay there, not thinking of the race ahead today but instead the man next to her now, and she didn't want the alarm to go off.

Of course it did.

Matteo groaned at the intrusion and pulled her closer into him.

Their temperatures matched, their muscles were loose and relaxed and she felt him slowly harden and the nudge of him at the back of her thigh, which seemed to Abby to be at odds with his regular breathing.

Her breathing wasn't in the least regular. She could feel his hand on her stomach and she lay locked in private thoughts and aching with want. She lay in a body that was finally ready to commit, next to a man who never would.

Abby turned over to face Matteo and his arms, even in sleep, moved to accept her.

He really was asleep.

All the tension from last night had left and his mouth was just a little open and she was so close to leaning over and kissing him awake, just giving in to and exploring the want that hummed through her now.

The snooze alarm went off and she watched his face screw up and his hand reached for a pillow, pulling it over his head and, in that moment, Hunter left every equation.

There were no more thoughts of revenge, no past to overcome, just the quiet of morning and a feeling of peace as she lay next to a man who plucked the strings of her heart.

Just that.

Abby rolled over and turned off the alarm and he pulled her back to his side. 'Matteo, I've got to go.'

He fought to wake and the events of last night

started to filter in. 'I'll walk you down,' he mumbled and moved to sit up.

'Stop it,' she said. 'I don't need a bodyguard.'

She just needed *him*; yet Abby knew Matteo had checked out on love.

'Go back to sleep.'

She went and had a quick shower and dressed in the clothes that he had fetched for her last night and then came back into the bedroom, where he lay awake now, looking at her. He looked sulky and angry and she knew why—Hunter was around.

'You're going tomorrow, Matteo. I'm here for a few more days, dismantling the car and then straight on to Monte Carlo, so it seems a bit stupid to be walking me to my room today.'

He said nothing.

Matteo didn't know what to say.

Abby was right—tomorrow at six in the morning he'd be gone and, more to the point, he had never been another's shadow.

Silence hung between them.

It wasn't a row; it was Check.

His heart was under threat of capture and Matteo didn't like that feeling in the least.

'Good luck today,' Matteo said but it came out in a rather forced voice.

So, too, was hers. 'Thanks.'

He lay there when she had gone. Yes, tomorrow

he would be back in Manhattan and, Matteo decided, he was going to go and get laid.

It had been…

He didn't really want to do the math. Matteo didn't want to admit that since their first dinner in Dubai, he'd lost interest in that half of the world population that had once been his playground.

No, he wouldn't be getting laid any time soon.

Matteo knew he was lying to himself. Instead the next couple of weeks were going to be spent stressing at the thought of her in Monte Carlo with that animal around.

He reached for the hotel phone.

Abby stepped into her hotel room to change into her lovely bottle-green outfit. She opened the chocolate that was on her pillow and as she popped it into her mouth she picked up the note that was beside it.

> *Dear Abby,*
> *You need new underwear. Shall I take you shopping or can I choose?*
> *Matteo*

And then her phone rang.

'Did you get my note?' Matteo asked.

She knew he was ringing to check that she'd got back okay, but it was nice that he didn't have to admit it.

'I did.' Abby smiled. 'You can choose.' And then

she was serious. 'Nothing's going to happen today, Matteo. All anyone is thinking about is the race.'

'I know and I meant what I said, even if I didn't say it very well—good luck today.'

'Thanks.'

Matteo had quite a morning in a very lavish boutique.

A few women nudged and laughed but he cared not and amassed quite a collection, which he asked to all be wrapped and then sent up to her room. Then Matteo had lunch and finally he took himself trackside.

The streets were packed and lined with spectators and when he finally made it to the Boucher sheds he, as always, stayed back, though Pedro stopped playing video games and came over and they chatted for a few moments.

Abby saw Pedro was smiling at something Matteo had said, and whatever her personal feelings were towards Matteo, she was very glad to have him as their sponsor. He was very good with Pedro, unlike the sponsor they had had last year who had demanded far too much, especially before a race.

But then, as the race commenced, there were no thoughts of Matteo, nor revenge—all Hunter was, was the car that was ahead of them.

As were eight others.

For the next two hours the team worked intently, working out the best refuel times. Matteo watched

Abby relaying instructions and giving Pedro some insights as to the cars ahead of him.

The Italian crowd were even more vocal than in Dubai and it was a loud, exciting couple of hours and by the last three laps Pedro had inched the car into fifth place.

Hunter's experience on the course showed, yet Evan pushed him hard and suddenly a roar went up as Pedro overtook into fourth.

Matteo found that he was chewing his nails.

And then it was into the final lap.

He looked over to Abby, whose face was pale but she was talking very calmly to Pedro through her mouthpiece, even though she must be feeling frantic. Hunter was well ahead of Pedro, Evan was in close second; it was a battle for third and, holy smoke, Matteo thought as Pedro accelerated out of the turn, he was going to get there.

Abby was right; this kid was a genius. The pale, sickly faced twenty-one-year-old that had climbed into the car, sure he would place last, got out a tri-umphant third, as the Boucher team cheered and embraced.

And no, Matteo wasn't on her mind right now because Abby nearly broke her neck just to get over to a jubilant Pedro.

'What the hell!' she screamed at him, her face split in a shocked smile.

'She flew!' Pedro roared back, simply elated. 'She just took off.'

And they were back to talking about the car as if she were a person. This third was even sweeter than placing first.

The press conference was very different to last time. Abby and Matteo were out and stood hand in hand as Hunter droned on and on about his experience. Evan, a man of few words, just shrugged when asked his predictions for the final race.

They were neck and neck—it could be any one of the three.

Pedro sat with a satisfied grin.

'We'll just have to wait for Monte Carlo,' was not just the gist but practically all Pedro said.

Yes, it was a different type of celebration tonight.

The Boucher team filled a gorgeous restaurant. Abby didn't have time to change but no-one cared. She had the best squid pasta she had ever tasted and Pedro made a speech and said that she, the car, was perfection.

It was wonderful; the party was moving on now to wild and Abby and Matteo decided to head back to the hotel but, before they did, Matteo pulled Pedro aside and had a word.

'Another shopping spree?' Abby checked but Matteo just shrugged.

Oh, he'd been speaking with Pedro but about

something rather more serious than shopping, not that he'd tell Abby that.

Yes, things felt different tonight and as Abby and Matteo got out of the elevator at the tenth floor Matteo reminded her of their deal.

'What happens when we make podium?' Matteo asked and, because there was no one around, he reminded her what happened with his mouth.

Hot and sexy, they were straight back to where they had been in Dubai as he kissed her up against the wall.

Only this time there wasn't the surprise element of his kiss, just hungry need, and she held his cheeks in her hands and kissed him back, her shoulders digging into the wall but her groin pressed hard into his.

It seemed miles to her hotel room and so they continued to kiss while walking—a hungry, laden kiss that had them tripping over a tray the next room had left out until finally they fell into her room.

'Hell,' Matteo said as he backed her to the door, undoing the black belt and buttons on her men's bottle-green trousers, and as he looked down he even laughed. 'This feels wrong...'

It felt pretty right to Abby.

He just kissed her until they stood, breathless and facing the other and both half-dressed.

'I'm not ready.' She was panting, feeling a tease but consumed with want.

'For what?' Matteo checked, slipping his hands

into her trousers and feeling her as damp as he knew she would be. He stroked her clitoris through her panties and resumed the kiss, probing her mouth with his tongue for a moment and feeling the tightening of Abby's thighs. He pulled back his mouth but not his hand as she simmered nicely.

Oh, Abby simmered. She wanted to, she wanted, wanted, wanted, but she was more scared of losing her heart than her control.

'How about a fashion show?' Matteo said and she glanced over his shoulder and saw for the first time all the parcels lying on her bed as his hand remained between her legs, his finger lightly stroking her and teasing her, while teasing himself, but then he removed it.

It was do up her trousers or take them off and Abby chose the latter.

'You're quite neat, aren't you,' Abby commented as he picked up her shoes and trousers and threw them in the wardrobe.

'A bit,' Matteo admitted. 'But I've made a lot of mistakes in my life and I'll scare the hell out of myself if I wake up tomorrow and see them by the bed.'

He made her laugh.

Matteo made her feel fine, just fine, to be wearing nothing except ugly panties and the dark green shirt.

She opened the parcels one by one as he did the same with the buttons to her shirt.

Some of the underwear he had chosen was the

colour of summer—gorgeous lemons and pale mint greens—while others were the shades of sin.

'Do you know why I chose those,' he said, having peeled off her shirt so she was down to her bra as Abby held some dark violet panties.

'Because they're crotchless?' Abby laughed when she poked her fingers through the hole.

'Actually, I didn't know they were,' Matteo said. 'I chose them because they're not just velvet on the outside.'

They weren't. The inside was just as soft and hidden-seamed.

'I thought they might feel nice.' Matteo explained his thought process.

Abby swallowed.

'Put them on.'

'I'm not ready to sleep with you, Matteo.'

He just shrugged and removed her bra so that her breasts dropped that aching inch and he toyed with her nipples, stretching them out. 'A lovely come would be nice though.'

He said it as if he were choosing from the restaurant menu, only some things weren't as easy as picking up the phone.

Or were they?

She thought of this morning—how turned on she'd been and how turned on she was now—and Abby handed herself over to him and nodded.

Even a little come would be a miracle!

Slut that Matteo was, the second that Abby nodded her consent he was happily stripping off and turning the heating up to rival Dubai at midday.

And then he told her that was his intention exactly! 'Remember that fashion show we had to sit through?' he reminded. 'I kept picturing you in all the underwear they were parading. Most uncomfortable half hour of my life…' He gave her a smile that had her nearly rock on her heels as she knelt on the bed. 'You were my Dubai fantasy—look how far we've come.'

Clearly they were here for the night.

He was almost clinical about it.

It was a very sexy clinic she was in though, Abby thought as Matteo chose a brandy from her minibar and then lay on the bed, naked, his erection lifting off his thigh, and she took her underwear and headed to the bathroom.

'Take some heels with you,' Matteo called.

Yes, look how far she'd come! Abby stood in the sexiest underwear in the world and added said heels. She even clipped up her hair and put on some lipstick.

It was a game to him and that helped Abby—why, she didn't know, but it just did.

Maybe because it was about fun, rather than Matteo throwing in sentiments that could never be met by the cold light of day.

And so she came out of the bathroom and as she

did, Matteo remembered the shy, nervous beauty who had walked out of the elevator in a silver dress.

That woman had gone for good now.

Abby stepped out and briskly walked the length of the room and then turned.

Nervous but not shy.

'They walk more with their hips,' Matteo said and took a sip from his bottle as she crossed the room. 'That's better, but more slowly.'

'Are you going to model for me?' Abby checked, strutting her stuff.

'Any time,' Matteo agreed and she looked at his erection and that he was playing with himself and her lips pressed together, wondering if she could ever lie there and do the same with him.

God, it was hot.

'Take off your bra.'

Even with double velvet her nipples were sticking out, and as she took off her bra he could see the spread of colour on her chest and that her stomach was taut with desire, and he could wait no more.

'Get here.'

She nearly ran.

To him.

Matteo guided her so that she sat on his stomach and he poured the last of the brandy onto his hand and then rubbed it into her breasts.

'The only way to drink brandy.'

She knelt over him as he made sure there was no

brandy left on the left. Abby's thighs were shaking, her neck was arched. One hand was on her hip as the other went straight for the kill. His hand slid past her exposed clitoris, leaving his thumb there while his fingers burrowed deep inside.

He changed breast.

She nearly lost her mind.

He just worked her as skilfully as she'd tune an engine. It hurt, the nicest hurt, and then he left her swollen, wet, slightly bruised breasts and his free hand started stroking himself again.

'Matteo…'

'I'm not going to.'

Abby's head lowered, just to watch them. Who was this woman, in obscene panties and loving it?

'Oh…' She just moaned as his fingers and thumb seemed to meet in the middle of a wedge of intimate flesh. He stroked her deep on the inside; he exerted pressure on the outside till her stomach seemed to meet her spine.

And yet, she couldn't—she let out a sob, borne of desire and frustration, and then felt as if she were choking, because everything in her tightened as Matteo started to come.

He had felt her tip—thank God, he thought, because it was past the point of no return, but he had never enjoyed himself more in the bedroom. Or anywhere else come to that.

Abby closed her eyes, regretting that she had no

choice but to, because the feel of him hot and pulsing against her was surely a sight to be seen as everything that had been missing spasmed.

Then she opened her eyes to the lovely sight of him pulling out the last of his come and then stroking it into her and she sank down on him rather than pull back. The intense feelings were better shared and then Abby sat back on her thighs and tried to drag in air.

Half an hour ago, she had glimpsed what it might be like.

Now she knew.

'What does it feel like,' Matteo asked, remembering the power of his own first come.

'Better than sex,' Abby said as he pulled her down, but to the side of him.

He knew how to do her right.

CHAPTER NINE

MATTEO WOKE FIRST.

They hadn't had much sleep.

The fashion show had continued until the early hours and they had pretty much done everything but make love.

Sex.

It felt like more than sex, even if they hadn't.

Whatever they had done, and they had done plenty, it had been amazing for both—oral sex had never tasted so good and Abby had just spent the last half hour before dawn, on her back, with Matteo's fingers over hers and, yes, she would sleep easily at night now.

But Abby wanted more than a part-time lover as her first and he respected that.

Matteo didn't like it but, yes, given that she had waited so long, he understood that she might want a little more than the occasional phone call, or the promise of more when he arrived in Monte Carlo.

The easiest thing now would be to turn off the

alarm, cancel the jet, kiss her awake and let her team start to work on dismantling the car, as he set to work on the walls that came between them.

Yet he lay there, staring up at the ceiling and remembering the promise he had made a very long time ago.

Oh, Matteo loved a gamble but as he looked over to where she was waking he knew that the stakes were too high.

He wasn't going to risk hurting an already damaged heart.

'You have to go?' Abby said.

She had woken to the pensive air and guessed he was wondering how to politely kiss and leave.

'I do,' Matteo said. 'And you've got a car to dismantle.'

Abby lay listening to Matteo in the shower and she knew she'd been right to hold back.

She didn't regret what had happened, but it did change things irrevocably.

There was an unfamiliar hollow feeling inside her because what had taken place last night felt very different this morning. There was little closeness now as Matteo came into the bedroom and quickly dressed.

'If you need anything for Monte Carlo…'

'We're pretty much sorted,' she said.

'Good,' he said. 'Well, if Pedro wants…'

'He's going to Rome with Bernadette for a few days,' Abby interrupted. 'The team will all be together again five days before the race.'

'I might not be able to get there until the day or so before.'

'Or an hour or so before,' Abby said.

'I didn't say that.'

'You didn't have to.'

'I'll just see what happens with work.'

It was a horrible end to a blissful night. He went to kiss her but she just turned her face away and, in truth, he was relieved she did.

He simply couldn't go through the motions with Abby, even in that.

Matteo was glad she'd insisted on no sex last night. He'd promised to sleep with her, no strings attached.

For the first time, Matteo wondered if he'd be able to.

It was surely better to stay back.

He didn't call.

Abby knew that he wouldn't. Matteo was a master at setting his boundaries, and that he wouldn't do relationships was his big one.

Somehow she had to accept that fact.

The circus moved on.

Pedro and Bernadette flew to Rome for some romantic downtime while the rest of the team went straight to Monte Carlo. Usually she'd be there, overseeing the car's arrival, but Abby had put it off.

There were a lot of bad memories in Monte Carlo; Matteo knew that and yet, still, he did not call.

He wanted to.

Or rather he wanted a life that had existed before April. One where the Lost Mistresses had been just an old tale that his grandfather had told. He wanted the life he had once led back—fast paced, lots of sex, not getting off to a memory.

Matteo was angry.

Every time he thought of calling Abby he would pull up the image of himself and his father coming out of a casino some thirty years apart and, if that wasn't enough of a reminder, the arrival of an email from Ellison was.

Any progress? Abby has formally declined my invitation.

Good for her, Matteo thought. It was Ellison's do the Friday after the race and he was tempted to reply to the email with two choice words.

Yet, he was as complicit in the attempt to get her to the function, wearing the necklace, as her father was.

Even Giovanni had called wanting an update and Matteo had been unusually terse with the old man.

Matteo knew that he had to speak properly with his grandfather.

Yes, he was angry.

Abby deserved better—someone who would deliver on the relationship front and, according to his lineage, Matteo never could. Even if by some miracle he could negate that fact, he knew that the moment Abby found out about the origins of his supposed interest in her team, it would end them.

Checkmate.

And so the day she got to Monte Carlo he fired one very rapid text.

Hope preparations are going well. I'll try to make it for the practice race.

And then he fired another text to Pedro, reminding him what they had discussed, and the best that Matteo could do was hope Pedro would take his request seriously.

Pedro did.

Abby hated being here.

She woke up and let out a tense breath as she checked her phone and of course Matteo hadn't called.

Only it wasn't just Matteo's imminent arrival that had Abby in knots.

Matteo had been right; Hunter was playing mind games because he'd changed hotels again and two days before the race had checked into the one that the Boucher team were staying at.

Yes, it was a different hotel than the last time she had been here, but just being in a hotel in Monte Carlo already had Abby on edge.

There was a knock at the door and it was the Perpetual Pedro wanting to go down to breakfast.

'I just want to run through a few things,' he said.

'Sure.' Abby nodded. 'I'll meet you down there.'

'I'll wait.'

'How's Bernadette?' Abby asked, because last night when Abby had headed back early from dinner, Bernadette had said that she had a headache and had joined Abby on the walk back to the hotel. Bernadette had even come up to Abby's room for a cup of tea and a chat about the press conference tomorrow and the practice race.

'She's doing great,' Pedro said.

'Good.'

Abby left Pedro in the corridor and grabbed her bag and then they headed down to the restaurant.

'Ready for the press conference?' Abby asked when they had been shown to their seats, and Pedro nodded but then he looked up and smiled, and Abby saw why.

Matteo was here.

'Hey!' Pedro said.

'How are you?' Matteo asked him.

'I'm confident,' Pedro said. 'Actually, I think I might take breakfast upstairs. Is that okay?' he checked with Abby and, as she nodded, it dawned on her then the reason Pedro or Bernadette had barely left her side.

'Did you tell him to watch out for me?' Abby

challenged as Matteo took off his jacket and took a seat.

'Yep.' He met her angry gaze. 'I'm not going to apologise.'

'What on earth did you say to him? You didn't tell Pedro...'

'Of course not,' Matteo said. 'I just told him that I'd had a couple of choice words with Hunter and that I didn't trust his temper. Pedro agreed with me!'

'He did?'

'Yep. He knows what a bastard he is.'

'I've been managing fine for the past eighteen months...'

'You weren't winning then,' Matteo pointed out.

He looked terrible, Abby thought.

There were black smudges under his eyes and she guessed he hadn't shaved for the best part of a week.

'What time's the press conference?' he asked.

'Eleven.'

'I'll stay for that and then I have to head off. I'm catching up with Kedah and we're going out on a friend's yacht. I'll be back tomorrow for the race but then I have to fly out straight after.'

'Matteo.' Abby took a deep breath. They hadn't even slept together and they were sniping and avoiding the other and so she told him what she had been building to since the morning he had left her hotel room.

'Can we just take it back to business?'

He closed his eyes and then nodded.

'You don't have to avoid me,' Abby said. 'Look, as much as you turn me on, I don't want to sleep with you.' She just said it, not knowing that the waitress was standing beside her waiting to take the breakfast order and then he laughed and said that he'd like his eggs sunny-side up please as Abby just about face-planted the table.

And then, just like that, they were friends again, but even as they smiled, there was, though, for Abby, something more that needed to be said. 'Matteo, thank you for the other night. I mean that. I have no regrets—it was amazing but...'

'There's always a but.'

'Not really. I know you don't want to take things any further and I get that. I respect that...' She gave him a smile. 'I don't have to like it.'

He liked that she was honest.

'I need more though.' Abby told her truth. 'I've waited a long time. Or rather I've been so messed up that I've missed out on an awful lot and I just want, well, when I do sleep with someone, it has to mean something.'

'I understand.'

'So thanks for the offer of a sex lesson but I shan't be taking you up on it.'

Matteo let out a breath of both relief and regret.

Relief that they were finished with.

Regret that they would never be.

'Are we good?' Abby checked and he took her hand and gave it a squeeze.

'All good.'

And so they stood, side by side, but not holding hands, as the stars of the show took their places.

It was the deciding race tomorrow and Evan, Hunter and Pedro were all a chance.

The winner would take all.

But though the desire to win burnt bright, it was no longer driven by revenge. There *was* next year, Abby thought.

It didn't all have to be now.

She wanted next year. More than that, she wanted the team she had built to all be together, but then a journalist asked Pedro the question that was on everyone's lips.

'Are the rumours true about you signing with the Lachance team next year?'

Pedro looked over to Abby and she gave him a smile and a very slight nod, letting Pedro know that he could answer with the truth—they had made a deal after all.

'I've been approached.' Pedro shrugged.

'And?'

'In fact, they asked to speak with me yesterday,' Pedro continued, 'but as I said to them—their cars are as dated as their drivers.'

There was a small stunned silence at the obvious

provocation and then the cameras started flashing and Hunter got up and walked out.

'Game on,' Matteo said.

The practice race went well and then Matteo disappeared to get ready for his night on the town. Abby had a lot of work to do on the car and so it was Perpetual Pedro who hung around.

'Go!' she said to Pedro when it was close to seven. 'I don't need a babysitter and you need to sleep.'

'Abby...'

'Pedro,' she warned. 'I have every right not to walk in fear and I'm exercising it. Go.'

Reluctantly, Pedro did and Abby worked till after ten, fine-tuning the engine till she was as happy as she could be with it and then she took a cab back to the hotel.

She was ready simply to go to bed and to do her best not to think of what Matteo was up to now that she had let him off the hook.

Abby climbed out of the cab, wondering if she could be bothered to get room service. The moment she walked into the foyer though, there was Matteo walking with Kedah, both looking like the two playboys they intended to be tonight.

Clearly they were just heading out.

Matteo had shaved and was wearing a suit and had that arrogant, rich gleam in his eye and he was, Abby knew, about to exercise *his* right to get royally laid.

'Abby?' He frowned as she passed them and he saw that she was alone. 'Where's Pedro?'

'In bed, where he's supposed to be before a race!' Abby angrily answered. 'Don't ever mess with my team and tell them what to do. You were supposed to be hands off, remember!'

'I was just…'

'Well, don't! It's not your job to look out for me and neither do you have the right to interfere with Pedro's build-up to the race.'

A car was waiting for them in the forecourt and as Kedah climbed in he waved to Matteo to get a move on.

'Your friend's waiting for you,' Abby said. 'Have a *great* night, Matteo.'

She just brushed past him, loathing herself for the anger and jealousy that had shot from her lips. He didn't deserve any of that. They had agreed to no-strings sex and she had been the one that had backed out.

What the hell was he supposed to do? Abby thought as she closed the door to her room and stripped off her greasy overalls.

She ran a bath and, as it filled, sat at her desk, trying to type up the adjustments she had made to the car but the figures all blurred before her eyes. There were emails she had to answer about order of events for after the race but all she could think about was Matteo and where he was right now. Then she suddenly remembered the bath.

Thank God for the overflow, Abby thought, and then she climbed in the overfull bath and cried.

For him.

For them.

And for the wish that she had at least slept with him.

Once.

Her first because, if not technically, Matteo would have been her first, and the way she felt about him it felt right that it be him.

It was his lack of feelings for her that hurt.

She lay in the bath and let the hot water relax her and over and over she topped it up and tried not to think about Matteo and Kedah in some sordid hot tub.

Bastard!

Except he wasn't.

He had been completely lovely with her.

She got out of the bath and it was close to one and she knew that she had to be up at five and was just about to take her robe off and climb into bed when there was a knock at the door.

And despite brave words that she was fine without a bodyguard, Abby felt a prickle of fear.

Matteo was out, Pedro would be asleep. She knew that because he was always in bed by seven the night before a race.

The knock sounded again and she was sweating, Abby realised. Her legs wouldn't move and she just stared at the door, too frozen to go to the peephole and see who it was.

'Abby?'

She just about dropped in relief when she heard Matteo's voice and wrenched open the door.

He saw her terror.

'I thought...'

'Sorry, sorry...' He took her straight in his arms. 'I should have called.'

'I thought you were on the yacht.'

'I couldn't get it up.'

He was so crude and yet he made her laugh.

'I didn't even try,' he admitted and then, because he was holding her, because they had missed each other, for even as his mouth moved to hers Abby was reaching for him and they kissed intensely, hurriedly, before logic moved in, before they thought of the many reasons they should not. His arm curled around her waist as he pulled her in. The fear that had gripped her turned to angry passion and as she kissed him back Abby pushed Matteo's jacket down and it fell to the floor. She didn't care about tomorrow when she could have tonight. 'Abby...' She was opening the buttons to his shirt, her mind made up, yet Matteo refused to give her even a moment to regret and he peeled his mouth away. 'I need to tell you something.'

'You don't.'

They were panting, both breathless, and she didn't

need to hear now that he didn't love her and never would.

'Abby,' Matteo said. 'You do deserve better than this.'

She did, because he was hard and his hands were bunched into the gown so as not to tear it off and they could be over and done with—Abby up against the wall, he could be taking her now—but he would not allow another morning between them like the last one, where the air was awkward and the conversation wooden. He would not do that to her.

'We need to talk.'

'Said the playboy.' And then she saw that he was in as much of a mess as she, Abby realised. 'Matteo, I don't need to hear it. I know we're going nowhere.'

'And I'm trying to tell you why it has to be that way.'

It was possibly the most responsible decision in his life and regrettable at that because there was so much energy and want between them that it felt almost criminal to pull back. His shirt was undone and damp from her wet hair but he took a seat beside the desk as Abby straightened out her robe and then took a seat at the desk in front of her laptop. 'It's like a doctor's visit,' he said and she smiled but they were both hurting so much that their smiles didn't last. 'I know you should be asleep but I needed to say this. I really do have to leave tomorrow straight after the race so if I don't say it now…'

'Are you drunk?'

'A bit.' He nodded. 'Look, you know how everyone says, "It's not you, it's me"?' he said and now Abby really smiled.

'Well, in this case it *is* me,' she said. 'I have more baggage...'

'No,' Matteo interrupted. 'It *really* is me.' He took a breath before continuing. He had never fully had this conversation in his head, let alone with another. 'I made a decision a few years ago...'

'You don't have to do this, Matteo,' Abby said because she could see his discomfort and reluctance to reveal more of himself.

'I want to though,' Matteo admitted. 'I know that you've got baggage and I don't want you thinking that my reluctance to get involved with you had anything to do with what's gone on between us, or that what's happened to you in the past has any bearings on my choice. You're right, you should hold out for someone who can give you all that you deserve and I truly can't. I don't want a relationship.'

'I know,' Abby said, yet there was this tiny part that hoped one day he might change his mind.

He answered it there and then.

'Ever.'

There wasn't even a sound as that little flame died; she just silently acknowledged its passing.

'My father had a lot of affairs,' Matteo said. 'I don't even know if you could call them affairs.

Just one-night stands, parties, drugs, alcohol...' He closed his eyes as he had to the drama all those years ago, but then he had been lying in bed listening to the fights; now he was doing his best to block out thoughts of a beautiful future with Abby. 'You never knew what you were going to get,' Matteo explained. 'I never knew who would be there in the morning—Mom, Dad, neither. Sometimes, for days on end it was just the nanny. Really, the older ones looked out for the younger...' He wasn't explaining this very well. 'I always knew that in the morning they might not be there. One morning they weren't but this time it was different. My grandfather was there as well as other relatives and outside there were reporters. But I knew already—I used to sleep with the radio on, I liked the voices and the music—I'd heard it on the news...'

Abby sat there.

She could remember the shock of her mother's death. It had been expected. She had been older but she could still remember the shock and finality of it.

Imagine losing both at five and to hear it read out as a headline on the news?

She tried to but couldn't quite grasp it.

'There was a huge funeral. The press were everywhere and it was on the television constantly, as I expected it to be,' Matteo said. 'It was the biggest news in my life and because I was five I actually thought that it *should* be everywhere...' He gave a wry smile. 'You know how small your world is when you're a child?'

Abby nodded.

'But then we went to live at my grandfather's and life went on but it had changed. The older ones all went off to boarding school and Allegra looked after my little sisters.'

'You?'

'I just did what I wanted and I was always getting into trouble but never really told off. I never got why my grandfather could hardly bear to look at me. No matter what I did, no matter how much trouble I got into, he hardly addressed me.'

'I thought you two were close.'

'We're not close, but we're closer now than we were.' Matteo nodded. 'While I was growing up he just stayed back. I started studying and after a year I realised I already knew how to make money. I had my start-up from my parents' estate, but I didn't need to sit in a lecture and be taught what I already knew and so I dropped out.' He looked up at Abby and he told her about a row that repeated in his head to this very moment. 'For the first time my grandfather got angry with me. We had a huge row. He told me I was wasting my life, I was heading for trouble and that he'd seen the signs, should have stepped in earlier...'

Abby swallowed.

'"But you didn't," I said to him. I told him he had never cared about me so why start to worry now? I told him that I knew he couldn't stand to be near me. I just didn't know why.'

Abby sat quietly, remembering Matteo's patience when she had told him what had happened in her past.

'My grandfather said, "Every time I look at you I see Benito."'

'Your father?'

Matteo nodded. 'He told me that I was just like him. A gambler, a liar, a risk-taker. He said that I was on track for disaster and he was tired of sitting back and watching history repeat...'

'Matteo.' Abby wouldn't buy it. 'Just because...'

'Abby,' Matteo interrupted her. 'I am *all* of those things. When my grandfather said what he did, it just confirmed what I already knew. I decided then that I would never let myself be like my father. Yes, I might have his traits but I won't get so involved with another that I'm capable of coming close to the damage that he did.'

'Matteo...' Abby started but then she halted herself. Matteo had let her speak; he had let her work out what she wanted for herself. It wasn't her place to tell him how he felt, even if she thought he was wrong to be so down on himself, but she did say a little. 'Your father had children and a wife—you don't.'

'And I intend to keep it that way,' Matteo said. 'He killed my mother. She had straightened herself out and his depravity and temper took her to an early grave.' And then Matteo did what he never had; he exposed his fear. 'I can't take that risk, Abby…'

'You're the biggest risk-taker I know.'

'Not with love.' Matteo shook his head. 'The stakes are too high. I'm sorry I can't give you what you deserve. I never set out for us to get involved, but then, on sight I did. For the past couple of months, since the day we met…'

She waited.

'It's been you,' Matteo said.

'Just me?'

'Abby, I might not be marriage material but it doesn't mean that I'm not crazy about you. I'm just here to explain why it could never last. I don't want to sleep with you tonight and for you to expect things to have changed tomorrow. They shan't have. I'm flying back and the next time I see you…' He shrugged, but it was a desperate one and Abby looked at a man who dealt in hours rather than days.

'Do you see why I had them pull up such a watertight contract? I'm good for business, not much else…'

'Matteo, I'm not holding out for a ring.' She wasn't sure at first what she was saying, but then Abby looked into the dark eyes of the man who had stayed loyal, who had listened, who had helped her work through dark, dark times to a point where a future seemed possible.

Even if it might not be with him.

And she was sure.

Very.

'I'm going to go,' Matteo said and he stood.

'Please don't.' Abby looked up at him. 'I heard the lecture…' Their eyes met. 'And I get it. I just want it to mean something…for us to mean something…'

'You know that we do.'

'And that's all I need to know.'

It was.

Whatever they had amounted to more than a time-frame, what they felt for the other might not ripen with age but could be celebrated now.

They kissed in a way they had both tried not to, slow, precise and affirming. A kiss that was so tender that the only place it could possibly bruise was your heart. And it punctured his because never, not once, had Matteo allowed himself to even glimpse what another with heart exposed might taste like.

'Sure?' Matteo checked but Abby had already jumped.

The haste in his breathing as her hands stripped him of his shirt had their mouths mesh in hot wet kisses that tasted of no holding back.

Abby's hands roamed his skin and pressed into his chest, feeling his tension and strength as he dealt with the last of his clothes. Haste left then; still kissing he undid her robe and she shrugged it off like a burden and wrapped her arms around his neck so their tongues could caress as their bodies met. His fingers strummed up her ribs and Abby rose to her toes just so that they might repeat that final ascent to the tender top again before he played her breasts.

And when his mouth lowered, when she ached for a bruising kiss, he just caressed one nipple with his tongue, over and over. Abby's knees wanted to give way, but she stayed standing, simply for more, till she bit back the urge to beg. So desperate for more that when his face returned to hers, his kiss drowned her demand and he led her to the bed.

Matteo's hand moved between her thighs and he played her so slowly, stroking her slick warmth, till her knees pulled up. She wanted to scream that she would not break. His skin, his scent, his want, did not match this slow perusal. He came over her and parted her legs wide. Abby met his navy eyes and she looked right at him as he first took her. She watched as he drove in slowly but as he met the depth of her desire, as welcoming muscles gripped, the crystal shattered for them both.

He kissed her eyes and her face; he moved to his side and turned her with him. Matteo stroked her thigh slowly and then down to her calf as he moved within. He positioned her leg higher and brought it onto his hip so he could thrust deeper.

Abby had given in trying to hide her feelings, and anyway there was nowhere to hide. She was moving with him, sharing intimate kisses, glad of his hands that pushed her hair back just so he could better see her come.

It felt like no other time; it *was* like no other time, because the feel of him swell inside her and the sudden haste in him had her sob as she tightened. Her thigh over his cramped but it only heightened the intensity as he parted her wider with deft hips that only angled to get him in deeper as Matteo came hard into her.

It left him dizzy; it made her the same. It was so intense that for a blind moment Matteo believed all things possible. He straightened her cramped limb; he bought her back down with a kiss—each pain he ironed, while still within, except for the big one.

And when he went to fix that, when in the rush of a high, he almost lost his head and told her the one thing she wanted to hear, Abby stopped him with a kiss, a hurried one, a necessary one.

Not for Matteo's sake, but hers.

No lies, no promises.

That it meant something precious was enough.

CHAPTER TEN

'You're not very good for my race preparation.' Abby sighed as she stretched her body and tried not to give in to temptation and sleep.

They hadn't slept, and if she did now, then she might just wake up to a call from Pedro to ask where the hell she was.

'I'm going to ring down for coffee,' she said, deciding caffeine was in order before facing the world. 'Do you want one?'

'No.' Matteo yawned. 'It will ruin the very long lie-in that I intend to have.'

'How long?' Abby groaned and pulled a face as, having briefly opened his eyes, Matteo closed them again as he spoke.

'Well, it's nearly five now and Kedah doesn't get here till around midday, so about seven hours...' he said, rubbing in just how little she had slept.

Yes, it was incredibly hard to peel herself out of bed but she did so and showered and tried to get her head into what had once been the most important day of her life.

It still was, Abby thought as she showered.

Last night made it more so but for different reasons.

By the time she came out, her coffee had arrived. Abby took it out onto the balcony and looked out to the beautiful old buildings and the sparkling Mediterranean and, yes, Monte Carlo truly was beautiful.

It matched her memories of it now.

And whatever happened from here on between herself and Matteo, she'd be okay. The last time they had awoken together it had been awkward and difficult. It wasn't now and Abby was determined to never let it get to that again.

She did not regret last night and surely never would.

It had been a very deliberate choice that she had made.

Abby went back in and Matteo was sleeping and so she dressed in her race-day bottle-green and then headed out to face the most important day of her life.

Her working life, Abby amended.

There was more now.

The build-up to the race passed in a blur.

Pedro was locked into his video games and Bernadette was doing her own thing, catching up with friends on her phone and present but not getting in the way.

She was good to have around, Abby thought.

Matteo and Kedah arrived just after one and there was a sense of calm in the Boucher camp.

Even if they came last they'd already won.

They were more united than they had ever been. Pedro was staying on and they had two amazing races behind them.

As the starting time to the final race of the Henley Cup approached, Pedro came out in his leather and he looked determined rather than tense. Bernadette gave Pedro a kiss for luck and everyone else wished him well but then it was just him and Abby for that last little talk before he took his place.

This time Pedro's teeth weren't chattering with nerves and there was no need to talk him down. Still, Abby carried on with what she had planned to say, that it was the taking part that counted and to remember how far they'd come. The Henley Cup would be the icing on the cake, she told Pedro.

'You always eat the icing first.' Pedro grinned as he put on his helmet.

'Okay, I lied,' Abby admitted and gave up on her losers-are-still-winners approach. 'Bring it home.'

It was a spectacular race. How could it not be? The scenery was straight from a travel brochure, the weather perfect and the car that Abby loved so took off like a bullet from the chamber and left half the field behind.

They were off.

Matteo juggled cola and binoculars as the cars took to the gorgeous hilly streets and then later wished that he hadn't had so much cola because, with only five laps to go, and the top five a close pack at that, he had to excuse himself, leaving Pedro in fourth.

Matteo returned to Kedah's side to be told that Pedro was now third.

The Lachance team and Hunter were first, the Carter team with Evan at the helm in close second.

Matteo glanced over to Abby and saw her concentration as she spoke into her mouthpiece.

Not a stolen glance between them.

And he loved that about her—her drive, her focus—and so he got back to watching the race but, as he did, something happened.

Not on the track.

Well, yes, something happened on the track, because Pedro overtook Evan but, as he did so, hope overtook fear for Matteo.

Just this quiet second in a noisy world where Matteo lost the dread that he never showed, or rather, his fears that he had shown only to one other—Abby.

And if Pedro won, he was going to do it, Matteo told himself.

He was going to somehow put everything right.

'Come on,' Matteo shouted and it felt like Pedro must have heard because, just past the final bend, Pedro not just overtook Hunter, he almost blew him off the track.

'Bring her home!' Matteo shouted and, yes, now even he was talking about the car as if it were a person.

She won!

It was delicious; it was chaos.

As Hunter tried to right the car, Evan screamed past and the Carter team took second place.

There was music and champagne and the cup held high and it was all just a gorgeous blur until it was time for the press conference.

Abby was trying to locate Pedro and found him talking with one of the organisers and so Hunter and Evan had already taken their places as the victor walked in to applause.

Abby stood to the side and Matteo, in the middle of the room, looked at her unreadable expression and wondered what was going on in her mind as the questions commenced.

'Congratulations to Pedro,' Hunter said. 'He's an amazing talent. Without him...'

Hunter looked directly at Abby and tried to tell her she was nothing, that were it not for their driver...

And Matteo watched as...no, she didn't struggle to breathe, and neither did she mouth an obscenity, or do any one of the things that she would be more than entitled to do.

There was more in her armoury than that.

Abby smiled.

For one reason only—she was happy.

And if looks could kill, then a well-timed smile could maim, because after the press conference, to Matteo's relief, Hunter's jet took off a lot faster than the Lachance car and finally there was this little moment when it was just Matteo and her.

'You beat him,' Matteo said.

'No.' Abby shook her head. 'We won.'

She wanted to better explain the change in her, the changes to her heart that he had helped make— to say that, even if there was no future for them, she would treasure the past for ever, but there wasn't time to do that now.

'Hey, Matteo...' Pedro shouted over. 'How about it?'

'How about what?'

'I just got permission, before they take the barriers down. Do you want that ride now?'

'Matteo has to head off,' Abby said, covering for him, as she knew that the very thought of a ride in a racing car made him feel ill, but then, as always, Matteo surprised her.

'I'd love to, Pedro.'

Matteo suited up and the face that disappeared into the helmet was grey but this was something he wanted—no, needed—to do.

Abby watched as he came out of the shed and her eyes drifted over his leather-clad body just as his had over hers that first day.

'Is it wrong to say just how much I fancy you now?' Abby asked.

'You're not doing it for me, Abby,' Matteo said and blew out a breath.

'You don't have to do this.'

'Oh, but I think that I do.'

He climbed in and took his seat and pulled down the harness and then Pedro did something—he came over and carefully checked Matteo's helmet and harness before getting in himself.

And therein was the difference.

Pedro was nothing like Matteo's father.

Pedro was an expert.

He trained for this, slept for this; every morsel that passed his lips was to better himself for this and Pedro kept to the rules.

And so, too, could Matteo.

Matteo wasn't his father either.

All those thoughts buzzed louder than the engine as Matteo found out firsthand just how fit you had to be to deal with the G-force and heat and demands on the body as the vehicle cornered, as well as that Pedro had to focus.

Yes, it was terrifying but exhilarating and it was one of the best experiences of Matteo's life, and as he climbed out it was to a world that looked different.

'I feel like I've laid a ghost to rest,' he admitted to Abby as he took off his helmet.

Abby nodded.

Last night, so, too, had she.

CHAPTER ELEVEN

As MUCH AS he had wanted to stay and join in with the celebrations, Matteo really did need to leave and head back to New York.

Even more so than before now.

With time differences and flying time, it felt odd that it was still Sunday, albeit late in the evening when he drove towards the Di Sione estate.

Giovanni had appointments all week and, if Matteo wanted to speak with him, then it had to be tonight.

Matteo had told Giovanni that he was coming and he knew that the old man would be hoping it was because Matteo had good news for him.

He wondered how his grandfather would take the news.

Alma let him in and said that Giovanni was in the lounge and Matteo thanked her and walked through.

Giovanni was sitting, staring out to the lake, and Matteo knocked on the open door to alert him that he was here.

'Matteo!' He turned and gave a smile of delight and went to stand but Matteo waved him down and went over and kissed him on the cheeks.

A pang of guilt hit Matteo when he felt the frail shoulders beneath his hands and saw his grandfather's tired, lined face.

'You've been busy,' Giovanni said.

'Yes, I have to say I like the motor racing world.'

'I see your team won the cup. I got up early and watched the race.' Then Giovanni's face grew serious. 'It's not good news, is it?'

It felt like good news to Matteo.

He was crazy about someone for the first time in his life but, no, there was no need for Giovanni to know all that.

'Not really,' Matteo said and he took a seat. 'I tracked down the necklace. It had been bought by...'

'Ellison!' Giovanni rolled his eyes. 'I guessed that much when I saw you with his daughter. I don't think you've ever been with a woman that long.'

'Her name's Abby,' Matteo said. 'And I've been sponsoring her team. When I first met with Ellison he said that he wanted me to get his daughter to a function that he's holding this Friday. If Abby's wearing the necklace, then it's mine.'

'And?' Giovanni frowned. He didn't see the problem. 'Surely she can wear it for just one night?'

'It's her mother's necklace,' Matteo said. 'Abby wore the necklace the night that her team placed first.

I'm sure it must mean a lot to her and I'm not going to take it from her.' He continued. 'I can't.'

'Even though you know it means everything to me.'

'Even knowing that,' Matteo said.

'You're in love?'

'I think so.' Matteo admitted as much as he dared, because love wasn't a place that he knew. 'What I do know for sure, though, is that I care about her and I'm going to do whatever it takes not to cause her pain.'

He was not his father's son, Giovanni realised.

Matteo was very much his own man.

'I hate letting you down.' Matteo continued to speak as Giovanni took the news in. 'I know that I told you I'd bring the necklace to you but, at the end of the day, I can't do that to her.'

Giovanni sat back in the chair and looked out to the lake. He wanted the necklace so badly. A part of him had hoped that finding the Lost Mistresses, and having them together again, might somehow heal his fractured family. And yet, while he ached to have the necklace that meant so very much back in his possession, maybe its magic had already worked. Giovanni had never heard his youngest grandson speak of anyone in this way.

'Could I see it again,' Giovanni asked. 'Do you think, if you explained things to Abby, that maybe she would let me hold it one more time?'

'I think so.' Matteo's response was cautious. 'The

thing is...' He blew out a breath. 'It might take a bit of time to get her to agree. I'm going to have to tell Abby that the necklace is the reason I first got in touch. If I know Abby at all, then that isn't going to go down very well.'

'You're going to be in trouble again.' Giovanni smiled.

'For sure,' Matteo agreed. 'Let me work on it.'

And work on it he did.

It was quite a busy few days for Matteo but he did make the time to call Abby and he could hear the surprise in her voice.

'I just wanted to see how everyone pulled up after the celebrations,' Matteo said.

'Well, I don't think anyone has pulled up yet,' Abby admitted. 'I don't think anyone's coming back to earth any time soon. We've got the big presentation and party in LA on Friday. You could come...' She tried to keep her voice light, to not build her hopes up that he had called her.

Actually, Matteo couldn't be there for the presentation in LA, not that he could tell her why.

'I can't make it on Friday. Will Hunter be there?' he checked.

'Nope,' Abby said. 'He's gone to ground.'

'Good. So when will you be back?'

'On Saturday afternoon.'

'Would you like to go out for dinner?' Matteo casually asked, as if he hadn't already booked the restaurant, as if all the plans he had made this week didn't depend on her response.

There was a long stretch of silence before she answered.

Long, because she hadn't expected his call and now an invitation to dinner on the very night she got back was a little more than she dared to glimpse.

He might just want to discuss the team, Abby attempted to warn herself, but her heart refused to be reeled in.

Oh, please don't hurt me, Abby thought.

Please don't get my hopes up high because I accepted a one-night stand when you said it could be no more than that.

'Yes.' Abby cleared her throat and did her best to sound as if it wasn't such a big deal. 'Dinner sounds great.'

'Saturday, then. Text me your address. I'll be there about eight.'

He didn't await her response; Matteo, too, was having trouble keeping things even.

On Friday he walked into a very exclusive jewellers.

'I've never worked so hard,' the jeweller said and when he showed Matteo the final piece Matteo could see the hours and skill that the jeweller had put into this masterpiece.

Even though the jeweller had only a photo to go on, it could have been made by the same designer!

The emerald sat up high on a platinum setting and it really was a work of art.

No, he hadn't had a replica of the necklace made.

You could never fully replicate the real thing.

And the necklace was the real thing, Matteo was very sure.

And so he'd had made a ring.

'I can't see anything on the photograph of the necklace to indicate origins,' the jeweller admitted.

'It's all a bit of a mystery.' Matteo was also bemused but his grandfather had remained unforthcoming.

'She's a very lucky lady,' the jeweller said as he nestled the ring into a box Matteo had had designed to match the case for the necklace.

'I might have to remind her of that,' Matteo said, imagining Abby's reaction when he told her the truth.

He was nervous to tell her about the necklace—of course he was—but with this ring...

He got back to his apartment and put the photo of the necklace and the ring in his safe and then lay back on the bed and tried to plan his speech for tomorrow. Matteo didn't get very far. He could never quite get past the bit where he told Abby that he'd stood in her father's study and come up with a plan to sponsor her, without imagining his face being slapped.

Deciding that he'd just have to wing it at dinner tomorrow, he dozed off.

Matteo woke to his phone buzzing and the sight of a skyline that was backed by a dusky pink sky.

'Abby?' he said, sitting up. 'What time is it there?'

'Eight,' Abby said and Matteo frowned because it looked as if it was evening and LA was a few hours behind them but then she explained. 'Matteo, I'm already in New York.'

'How come?'

'Hunter arrived this morning and—do you know what?—I just didn't want to be around him. It's Pedro's night and I don't want anything to get in the way of that and so I decided to head for home.'

'Good.'

'I need a favour,' Abby continued. 'Well, I don't need one but it would mean a lot if you could do this for me.'

'Name it.'

'I'm on my way to my father's...' Abby took a breath. 'I know I said that I wasn't going to go but I've changed my mind. It's not such a big deal. I'm just going to put my head in for a couple of hours. It would be great if I could say that you were coming too.'

'Abby.' Matteo was already off the bed. 'I'll come with you. I'll just get changed and then I'll pick you up.'

And 'fess up!

He was already undoing his belt as he spoke but speed wasn't going to save Matteo.

'No, there's no need for that,' Abby said. 'He wants me there by eight and I'm already running late. Look, I get it if you don't want to come but it would help a lot if you could. I'll text you the address…' She looked out of the window of the car and saw that she'd arrived. 'I'm here now. Wish me luck.'

It really had been a last-minute decision.

Abby had arrived home and opened up her case and had seen the gorgeous silver dress that she had worn on the night they had won in Dubai.

Why not? Abby had thought.

She had pinned up her hair to show off the necklace to full effect and had just decided to play the game for one night.

No, she had long ago realised her family would never be close but surely an occasional function or get-together was doable.

Now the car that her father had sent for her pulled up at the house that had never really been a happy home and the door was opened for her.

It had been years since Abby had last been here.

Emails and the occasional phone call had been all she could manage since that terrible time, sitting in her father's study and being told Hunter wouldn't be called to answer for his actions.

She was ready to put it all behind her and, nine years on, Abby felt a lot more together and capable than the last time she had walked up the stairs to the entrance of her family home.

'Abby!' Cries went up from everywhere as she entered.

'Congratulations' were offered from all directions, as well as, 'Wow, look at you!'

'Abby!' Her sister, Annabel, came over and gave Abby a kiss on the cheek but it felt like a sting. 'You changed your mind about coming?'

'I did.'

'The prodigal daughter returns triumphant!'

Abby could have given a bitchy retort. She guessed Annabel thought she was only here to gloat because her team had won but, no, it had nothing to do with that.

'Just try and behave tonight,' Annabel said. 'This is important for Daddy.'

Annabel's husband came over and gave Abby a very guarded smile. 'Abby.'

Aside from that frosty greeting the night went well. Her father was too busy chatting people up to pay Abby much attention, which suited her fine.

Abby's phone buzzed and she saw that it was Matteo texting her.

I'm on my way.

She fired a text back.

No rush.

And then Matteo sent another.

Abby, we need to talk.

Abby frowned at the second text and then wondered if Matteo was doing one of his *I don't do relationships* things, and was maybe annoyed that she'd asked him to come. She decided she would explain when he arrived that this really wasn't a meet-the-father moment.

She was soon distracted when one of her father's friends called her over and asked about the race in Dubai.

'It was amazing,' Abby said for perhaps the fiftieth time that night but she was more than happy to talk about it. Realising that Matteo would be here soon she went upstairs and took a moment to refresh her make-up and check her hair and then stepped back and looked in the full-length mirror.

Yes, the necklace and dress worked but it was the woman wearing them who felt so different tonight.

She remembered coming down in the elevator and the smile on Matteo's face when he saw her and the wonderful times they had shared and she simply couldn't wait to see him again.

Abby went to head back down to the party. Oh, she would never be one who loved these types of events but she was glad that tonight she had made the effort. She felt confident…

Happy.

For the first time she could remember she felt

happy, confident and beautiful in her own skin and then she looked over and saw the man who had made all three possible walk into the Ellison home.

He was wearing a smart suit and his black hair flopped forwards and he brushed it back with his hand as he stood for a moment looking around, Abby guessed, for her.

'Matteo!' Her father saw him and Abby frowned at how pleased her father seemed to be that he was here.

Of course they would know each other from similar functions but it was a very friendly handshake that he gave Matteo. Her father even patted him on his shoulder and, as Abby walked down the stairs, she watched as her father and Matteo disappeared into his office.

Matteo had very much been hoping to speak with Abby before her father but, without that chance, he followed Ellison in, determined to have his say.

'Congratulations,' Ellison said.

'It was an amazing win,' Matteo agreed and then he looked to the photos Ellison had walked him through on the day they met and anger grew in his stomach. There was the photo of Hunter with Abby and this bastard knew what he had done to his daughter and yet still had that photo on the wall.

'I'm not talking about the win,' Ellison said. 'I was referring to your achievement in getting Abby here. I have to hand it you—I thought she might come tonight, albeit reluctantly, but she's been the belle of the ball. The necklace is yours... You've certainly earned it.'

Abby stood at the ajar door and somehow stayed standing as the floor seemed to disappear from beneath her.

What achievement?

It didn't make sense.

Yet it was starting to.

Her father had wanted her here tonight wearing the necklace and she knew—oh, yes, she knew—how low he could stoop.

Why had she thought better of Matteo?

Because, despite clear warnings, she'd gone and fallen in love.

She was tempted to turn, to just walk away and pretend she hadn't heard what was said and to simply make it through the night without creating a scene. It had nothing to do with the fact she was on strict instructions to behave tonight; it was more than that—she didn't want the dream to end.

The dream that Matteo had actually cared about her.

She thought of her mother, smiling for the camera, pretending all was well in a messed-up world, and Abby refused to let that legacy live on.

'What did you just say?' Her voice was very clear as she walked into the study. Matteo's back was to her but she saw it stiffen at the sound of her voice.

'Abby...' he started but Ellison spoke over him.

'I was just congratulating your sponsor,' Ellison said, not remotely bothered that they'd been over-heard.

But then, Matteo thought, if he was insensitive enough to have Hunter's photo on his wall, what was another layer of hurt to add to the mix.

'What does my wearing my mother's necklace have to with this?' Abby asked. She had walked right over and stood aside the two men and confronted her father first. 'What do you mean when you say that the necklace is Matteo's?'

'Can we talk away from here?' Matteo suggested.

'Why?' Abby checked. 'I think here is the perfect place. Why spread my misery outside the grounds of this home.' She asked the question again, her voice rising. 'Why would you tell Matteo that my neck-lace is now his?'

'It's actually *my* necklace,' Ellison corrected. 'Your mother left it to me. I knew that you needed money, Matteo wanted the necklace and I said if he could get you here wearing it for the do...' Ellison shrugged. 'It's no big deal.' As Abby's eyes filled with tears Ellison misread them. 'Oh, don't go get-ting all sentimental, Abby. Your mother loathed that necklace.'

'And I know why she did!' Abby was shouting now. 'Because, yet again, you'd been unfaithful and, yet again, you thought another trinket would put things right.'

'And it did,' Ellison said. 'Your mother knew how to behave, as does Annabel. Whereas you, Abby...'

'Whereas I,' Abby interrupted, 'don't simply turn a blind eye to everything!'

'Abby,' Matteo said. 'I can explain.'

'No,' Abby said. 'I don't want your charming lies. I want to hear—' her voice was rising further '—the truth from my father. At least *he* doesn't sugarcoat things.'

'Abby,' her father warned. 'Keep your voice down.'

'Then give me an answer. Are you telling me that you bribed Matteo?'

'It was a gentleman's agreement,' Ellison said.

'I've got this, thanks,' Matteo said to her father and taking Abby by the arm he tried to steer her away but she shook him off.

'And this gentleman's agreement happened... when?' Abby demanded.

'Matteo came and saw me in April to purchase the necklace...'

Hearing that a meeting had taken place even before she had met Matteo, Abby didn't need further details; she was already walking off. She had nothing, *nothing*, left to say to her father, and she had just one parting line for Matteo as she brushed past him.

'Screw you!' Abby said.

She stepped out of the study and walked briskly

towards the entrance and out the front door. Guests were staring and Annabel was throwing fire with her eyes as, yet again, Abby created a scene.

'Will you stop?' Matteo called as he ran down the stairs after her and then overtook. Abby stood on the bottom step as Matteo reached the ground and so he was right in her face but she just stared coolly back, refusing to break down.

'I hate you.'

'No, you don't.' Matteo took her arms and almost shook her to listen to him. 'You hate what I've done, you hate that I set out to deceive you, but I never have.'

'How can you say that when you met him in April? You were never interested in my team.'

It was simple maths to Abby.

From the very start Matteo had never been interested in her.

All the joy, all the memories, dissolved like soap left in the bathtub.

She remembered sitting in jeans in a stunning restaurant and the joy that it hadn't seemed to matter. Oh, there was a reason he hadn't cared what she wore—Matteo had had other things on his mind that night.

Was the necklace the reason he'd been prepared to take things so slowly?

She felt sick with recall as every sweet memory of them soured.

'Abby.' Matteo would not give in. 'My grandfather is sick and more than anything he wanted the necklace. I was going to pose as...'

'Pose,' Abby sneered. 'You started lying even before we met.'

'Yes, but I *stopped* lying an hour after we met,' Matteo said. 'You know that! By the next morning I was already head over heels with your team and by the next week I was struggling because I cared more about you than them...'

'Leave me alone.'

She was humiliated, embarrassed and more hurt than she knew how to be.

'I've been trying to tell you about the necklace...'

'When?' Abby demanded.

Matteo blew out a breath. He knew that he hadn't really tried; he had left it in the too-hard basket, it would seem, for too long.

'Have it...' Abby said, yanking off the necklace, and she tossed it at him but it clattered onto the ground. 'Take it to the old bastard. Tell him he's got his precious necklace now. I hope you're all happy.'

Matteo stood as Abby picked up the hem of her dress and walked briskly off.

He had a ring in his pocket but, no, some trinket wasn't going to fix this and maybe full disclosure might prove too little too late but nonetheless he went after her. 'If you think the past three months have been a sham…' Matteo started but Abby was too angry to let him speak.

'That's exactly what they have been. A sham. And you're the biggest sham artist of the lot.'

'I can't believe you won't even hear me out.'

'I don't *need* to hear you out,' Abby shouted. 'You're all the same!'

Even as she said it, even before Abby saw the expression on Matteo's face as the words hit, she wished she could scramble on the floor, not for the necklace but to retrieve her own words.

'Don't you *dare* compare me to them!'

And when she had every right to be angry—furious, in fact—she saw his anger. But it didn't scare her—in fact, it shamed her as Matteo continued.

'Don't you ever put me in your father or Hunter's league…' He was sick to death of it. He was sick of being blamed for others' mistakes and tired of being compared to his father. 'I would never knowingly hurt you.'

'You have hurt me though,' Abby said as tears started to fall.

'It's called a row, Abby…'

'And I don't need it!' She walked off to her car and, now furious himself, Matteo stood there and let her leave.

'Problem?' Ellison walked down the steps and retrieved the necklace and held it out to Matteo as he spoke. 'That's Abby—drama as always. Still, you kept to your end of the deal. You've got what you wanted.'

Matteo said nothing as he pocketed the necklace. It was far safer.

But instead of getting into his car, he took the steps in three strides and, with Ellison following, he walked back into the home and straight into the study from where they had just come.

'What do you think you're doing?' Ellison asked as Matteo ripped the photo of Abby and Hunter from the wall and smashed it over his knee. Not content with that he took out the image and he shredded it over and over and then tossed the pieces at Ellison.

'What you should have done years ago.'

But shredding a photo of Hunter wasn't enough for Matteo.

It was far from enough!

Matteo got in his car and drove, not to Abby's but towards the airport and, as he did, he summoned his jet.

'Now!' Matteo roared and then having ended the call he threw his phone out of the car window.

The bastard was in LA.

Oh, this had nothing to do with making things right.

This was just about catching up on so many un-attended wrongs.

CHAPTER TWELVE

ABBY WOKE AFTER MIDDAY.

Like a sad Miss Havisham she was still wearing her silver gown and her face was all swollen from crying till dawn.

Matteo hadn't come dashing to her door to explain, when she had hoped he might, but Abby understood why.

And he hadn't answered his phone when she'd tried several times to ring, and she understood why too.

She had put him in the same league as her father and, worse than that, Hunter, and that was the very last place he deserved to be. To a man like Matteo, who had been put in the same league as his father his entire life, it had been a very low blow she had served.

Abby simply didn't know how to put this right.

Yes, he had lied to her, but now, every time she got cross, every time a rush of anger rose, she remembered his kindness, his sexiness and how he had helped her to find herself.

She had everything she thought she ever wanted.

The Henley Cup.

A winning team.

Revenge.

Her sexuality back.

But not him.

No wonder he didn't want a relationship, Abby thought, only she tried one more time to reach him on his phone.

It was the Monopoly of love because she got sent straight to voicemail.

'Matteo, it's Abby. Last night…' She'd taken the low road. 'Last night,' Abby attempted again, 'I said some things that you didn't deserve to hear. I'm sorry for that and…' What else? Abby thought. The truth. 'I don't know what else to say. You're right, I can't believe that I didn't hear you out. I want to though.'

She rung off and sat there, then pounced on her phone when a text came through but sagged when she saw it was just Bella.

Have you heard the news? :-)

Abby frowned.

What news?

Turn it on.

Abby did and saw the serious face of a news reporter standing outside the venue where she was supposed to have been for the presentation last night. The reporter was talking about the tight-knit world of the racing community and denying that Hunter had been loaded and got behind the wheel.

'The Lachance team manager insists that he fell…'

And then they flashed to an image of Hunter leaving a medical centre and Abby swallowed because if he *fell*, then it must have been from some considerable height and in several directions!

She called Bella.

'What the hell happened?' Abby said. 'Did he take out a car?'

'Oh, this was no car accident,' came the gleeful reply. 'Your lovely sponsor paid him a visit last night.'

'Matteo?'

'Yep.'

'Oh, no…' Abby felt sick. 'Has he been charged?'

'That's just it—Matteo *wants* to be charged!' Bella laughed. 'In fact, when he'd finished with Hunter he took out a business card and dropped it on him and said that he was looking forward to explaining his actions in front of a judge. Oh, Abby, it was one of the best nights of my life. We're all still drinking and cheering.' But then Bella was serious. 'Hunter came on to me once. God, Abby, don't ask but…'

'It's okay,' Abby said. 'I get it.'

They would talk properly some day.

'Where is he?' Abby asked.

'Having his teeth reimplanted, I think.'

'No, I mean, where's Matteo?'

'I don't know,' Bella answered. 'He just left afterwards and no one knows where he is…'

Abby did.

As she rung off she heard the door and then his voice and there, swaying in the doorway, looking rather the worse for wear, was Matteo.

'I know you hate violence…' he started.

Abby did.

'But he had to pay.'

Matteo had a black eye and bruised knuckles and a chipped front tooth. It would have been some fight; Abby knew how hard Hunter worked to stay in shape and she also knew, firsthand, how violent his temper could be.

'Come in,' Abby said and she held the door open but Matteo shook his head.

'Nope, I'm just here to tell you one thing. Two actually.'

'Well, can we at least do that inside?' Abby asked and finally Matteo nodded and in he came. She spoke first. 'I tried to call you.'

'I threw my phone out the car.'

'Why?'

'Because I didn't want you to talk me down,' Matteo said, 'which you would have tried to and then you'd have worried all night.' Then he was more direct. 'And I was cross with you.'

She'd thought that he might be.

'What Hunter did to you was despicable. What he's still doing to you, you shouldn't allow. Stop wasting your life exacting revenge.'

'I know that now.' Abby was trying not to cry. 'Even when we won the cup, I kept wanting to explain that I was happy, just that we'd won, not because of beating him.'

'Good,' Matteo said and then he gave in standing and went and took a seat on a large dark sofa.

He looked around her apartment and, after the night he had had, it was nice and relaxing just to sit in silence. There must be a huge tree outside because the only view he could see as he stared out was green leaves.

'I'll get to the second thing in a moment,' Matteo said and rested his head back for a while.

'Can I get you anything?' Abby offered.

'A drink.'

She guessed he didn't mean coffee.

'I don't think you should be drinking,' Abby said but then went and poured him a very nice cognac.

'I thought you didn't drink,' Matteo said, taking a long, slow sip.

'I run a motor team,' Abby said. 'They get tired of lemonade. Actually, my friend Bella gave it to me when we came fifth last year. I've been hiding it from them since then.'

'Good.'

But the small talk didn't last for very long.

'Second thing,' Matteo said and he watched as her cheeks went pink and her eyes, which were still red from crying all night, blinked a few times. 'Don't ever again compare me to him.'

'I'm really sorry for what I said.'

'And so you should be,' Matteo responded, 'because I would never treat any woman that way.'

'I get that, Matteo. I was cross, I was upset...'

'No excuse!' he said and he pointed his finger at her. 'Because I love a good row but if you ever hurl that at me again I'll be straight out of the door.'

He served her a very serious warning but even as he did there was this little thing called hope flickering in her heart because...did that mean that they might, just might, have a future?

Oh, not a big one, he'd made that very clear, but he'd lived in her heart for three months yet and she didn't want it all to end on a row.

'And you're never to compare me to your father either.'

'I won't,' Abby said.

'He knows what happened?' Matteo checked. He still couldn't believe it but Abby nodded.

'He just carries on as if it didn't. I hate how he has that photo still on his wall.'

'It isn't any more. I smashed it.'

'Thank you.'

'And I tore it up into a million pieces and it still wasn't enough and so I went and found him and I don't regret it.' Matteo stood. 'I'm going to go.'

He wanted a bath and to tidy up; this wasn't how today was supposed to be.

'Don't go yet.'

'I'm a mess. I want to sleep.'

'I'll run you a bath,' Abby said. 'And you can sleep here.'

She just could not stand another twelve or twenty-four hours', or even, knowing Mattco, several weeks' delay in proceedings.

Abby ran him a bath and he stripped off as easily as he always did and got in and then she sat on the edge in her gown.

'Why are you still wearing it?' Matteo asked.

'I fell asleep with it on.'

'That's very un-Abby.'

'Yes, lately I am.'

He had the loveliest body and she got a very nice view of the best of it as he lay back and ducked his head under the water for a moment and then came up again.

'I know you don't want to hear it,' Matteo said, 'but I am going to explain my version of things.'

'I do want to hear it.'

'Then get my jacket.'

She did and he half drenched it as he went through the pockets and took out the necklace and then dropped his jacket back on the floor.

'You know my grandfather brought us up?'

Abby nodded.

'And I told you about the fight. How, since then, we've worked at things. We don't talk about much, but we do talk. I take him out and I care very much for him. In April he asked me to come and see him and told me that he was very ill.'

She knew that much from his conversation with Allegra.

'When we were growing up he used to tell us this tale about the Lost Mistresses. I never really paid much attention. He'd just say it all the time...'

'Tell me.'

'Oh, no...' Matteo rolled his eyes and put on an old man's voice. '"Don't ask me how I came by them...an old man must have his secrets..."'

Abby laughed.

'Well, he started going on about his Lost Mistresses again. He said he wanted me to find one of them for him. At first I thought he was a bit confused. But no, he showed me a photo of the necklace and said he wanted to go to his grave in peace and he begged me to find the necklace. I tracked it down to your father and I made him an offer, which he refused. Your father said that if I wanted the necklace I had to get you to come to his fundraiser, looking like a woman for once and wearing it.' He looked over to Abby. 'I should have said no then. It was wrong of me, I accept that. I told him that I wasn't going to seduce you or anything. He suggested that I go in as an investor.'

It hurt to hear.

She couldn't polish his words up like a stone.

The very first time they met he had lied to her.

'I thought you were interested in the team,' Abby said…and it sounded so pathetic, but not as pathetic as admitting, she had hoped, almost from the start, that he had wanted her. 'You said…'

'Abby, I hated cars. And you know why.' She nodded. 'But I didn't by the time we went to dinner.'

Still, she recalled him saying how great she looked in those awful jeans and the ease he had put her at.

To know it had all been a lie hurt like hell.

'Abby, I thought you were the rudest woman I'd ever met. I had a hangover, and your attitude made it very easy to walk away. I was going to tell my grandfather there was no chance, or make your father a better offer. But the moment we started talking, I mean, really talking, I was in. I wasn't pretending any more.'

'Yet you still didn't tell me,' Abby said, and she wasn't cross, just confused.

'When?' Matteo demanded. 'When was I sup-posed to tell you?' And then he told her something about himself. 'I'm a good liar, Abby, and I don't usually have much of a conscience. I say what I have to to get what I want and I'm very good at avoiding things. When my parents would fight I'd just go off into my own world. When my grandfather tells me he's dying, I suggest we go out for a drink. When the woman I'm crazy about tells me all that's happened to her and then comes down, so shy and nervous and wearing that necklace…should I have told you that night?' he asked. 'Would you have taken it well then?'

'No.'

'On Sunday night, as soon as I landed back in New York, I went and spoke with my grandfather,' Matteo said. 'I told him that he wasn't getting the necklace, that I wouldn't do it to you.' He handed it to her. 'It's yours.'

'Technically it's yours,' she said. 'Gentleman's agreement and that.'

'Your father's no gentleman, so that nulls that. It's yours.'

Abby took it. 'What did your grandfather say when he found out he wasn't getting it back?'

'He was upset, I guess, but he'll live.' Matteo closed his eyes. 'Actually, he won't.' He gave her a half smile. 'He asked if he could see it one more time—is that okay?'

'I think we could manage that.' Abby stood.

'Do you get now why I didn't tell you?'

Abby didn't answer him; instead she stood and walked to the bathroom door.

'You're going?' Matteo said.

'Yep.'

Matteo lay back in the water and closed his eyes again.

Of course she was.

CHAPTER THIRTEEN

ABBY WENT INTO her bedroom and the same tree that filled the view from her lounge was there in her bedroom window.

They could never end on a row.

In a few days the bruises would be gone, that gleaming smile would be back in place and Matteo would be off to pastures new.

Now though, even if he had lied to get past the locked door to her heart, she was very glad that he had.

In the past few weeks she had opened up and become more trusting, less wary. Matteo was right— had he told her then she would have walked away.

She had changed.

Everything had changed.

Right down to the fact that she took off her dress and she put on the necklace and then naked, save for the Lost Mistress, she walked back into the bathroom.

She loved him.

He had stood up for her, fought for her, and completely he accepted her and she accepted him.

Not quite perfect.

She wouldn't have him any other way.

For however long they had.

Abby didn't want to change him, nor for Matteo to change for her. She just hoped that one day he might lose his dark self-image and know the amazing man he was.

He was lying, dozing in the steamy water, but he opened his eyes when she walked in.

Yes, that shy nervous beauty had gone, as had that guarded woman, yet her eyes were a bit wary, no doubt wondering as to her reception as, for the first time, she initiated things.

'Do you be naked, Miss Abby?' Matteo said in a servant's voice and he held out a hand and helped her into the bath.

'Enough of that talk, young Matteo,' Abby said and any trace of awkwardness evaporated like the steam from the water as they made each other laugh. She sat between his big long legs as he eased himself up and she just wished they could stay in the bath for ever and that he would never have to leave.

'Oh, and you be wearing that lovely necklace,' he said. 'Can I feel your jewels?'

'You can.'

His hand slipped under the water.

'That's a fine one there,' Matteo said and he watched her bite on her lip.

God, it felt good, Abby thought as he moved deeper inside and his legs hauled her closer towards him.

'Can I show you something, Miss Abby?' Matteo asked and she could only guess what it was.

She was wrong.

'Lose the voice,' Abby begged. She didn't want to play servants any more and, as she climbed on, Matteo completely forgot he'd been about to produce a ring.

They couldn't kiss, given his swollen mouth, and so she just held on to his shoulders and moved on him at whim and then bent her head and bit him on the shoulder and wished, how she wished, she'd seen it in Dubai.

His fingers now dug into her buttocks and he said words that were going to really hurt her later, because he told her that he loved her.

'And I want to be with you for ever,' Matteo said.

He was a liar, Abby knew. He would say anything to win, and of course he did, as he pulled her down harder and faster. She was coming, and as he came he told her he loved her again.

'You don't play fair,' Abby said, her head on his shoulder, feeling the last flickers of them, and then she pulled back and looked at the most complex man she could meet.

'Can I show you something, Abby?' Matteo said in his lovely, normal voice.

'Yes.'

'You have to get off,' he said and, as she did, he added, 'While you're up…'

He made her, dripping wet, get out of the bath and into his jacket.

'I was going to show you this before you so rudely interrupted me,' Matteo said as she took out a small wooden box that was different, yet somehow the same, as the one she knew.

'What this?' Abby asked, opening the catch, and what she saw had her body tingle with goose bumps.

'What does it look like?'

'My necklace,' Abby said. 'Except it's a ring.'

It was the most beautiful emerald that she had ever seen, and the setting was the same as the necklace that they had fought over.

The necklace that had brought them together, even if it had torn them apart for a while.

'You had this made for me.'

'No,' Matteo said. 'I was walking past a shop… Yes.' He stopped teasing her. 'I had it made for you when I got back from Monte Carlo. I was going to tell you about the necklace and your father, tonight, in fact, and then I was going to give you this…'

How badly she had judged him.

She went to slip it on to her middle finger but it was too small.

'It's not a dress ring, Abby…' Matteo said and there was no tease in his voice. 'It's an engagement ring.' All joking was aside. He was as nervous as he'd expected to be, not because of what he was asking her—Matteo knew what he wanted. He was nervous that his past, that his father, that the doubts his own grandfather had about him, that he had had about himself, might have crept into her.

'You want to marry me?' She couldn't quite believe what she was hearing.

'More than *want* to marry you,' Matteo said. 'I have to have you in my life. I was going to ask you tonight.'

'I thought it was just dinner.'

'Just dinner?' Matteo checked. 'Or did you want sex too?' he said and Abby smiled as he pulled her back into the bath.

'I wanted sex too,' Abby said.

'And?' Matteo pushed.

'Some more time,' Abby said but then she looked at Matteo and days, weeks or months could never have been enough. 'I hoped for more but I never dreamt of this.'

'Dream bigger, then,' Matteo said. 'And when you can't, then I'll do it for you.'

He always had.

EPILOGUE

'ABBY!' MATTEO WAS very firm. 'You don't have to give the necklace to him. It was your mother's.'

'I want your grandfather to have it though.'

They were in his car, outside the Di Sione mansion, and Abby took the necklace out of its box and held it in her hands. She looked at the stunning emeralds, the colours that she had based her racing team on, only the necklace wasn't her mother. She didn't need jewels to remember Anette.

'I can remember the arguments,' Abby said with a wry smile. 'Not the one where he gave her this, but that was what my father did time and again. As beautiful as this necklace is, there weren't many happy memories attached for my mother. I know she'd be thrilled to make your grandfather happy. Clearly it means an awful lot to him.'

'It does,' Matteo said. 'I don't really know why.'

'Why don't you ask him?'

'One day,' Matteo said.

Except those days were running out, Matteo

thought as Abby carefully placed the necklace back into its box.

'Come on,' Abby said.

'You're sure you want to do this?' Matteo asked.

Only he wasn't asking about the necklace this time.

'I'm certain.'

It had been two weeks since that terrible row when they'd both thought they had lost everything.

These were different times now.

Matteo knocked and then he let them into the house he had grown up in and smiled to Alma, who was walking towards them and beaming.

'You look beautiful,' she said to Abby and then she looked at Matteo. 'You've shaved!'

'I have.'

'Signor Giovanni's all ready for you,' Alma said. 'He's in the main lounge. Shall I let him know that you're here?'

'No.' Matteo shook his head. 'We'll go straight through.'

Matteo was nervous, wondering how his grandfather would react, not just to the necklace—Abby was the first woman he had brought to his grandfather's home.

'Matteo…' Giovanni went to stand but Matteo told him to save his energy and went over and kissed him on both cheeks.

'Nonno, this is Abby…'

'Abby Ellison,' Giovanni said. 'Owner of the Henley Cup. Congratulations! That was an amazing win.'

'Thank you.' Abby smiled and decided that she liked him.

When she had heard that Giovanni had compared Matteo to his reckless father and had caused Matteo so much pain and to doubt himself, she had been cross with the old man. Now though, she had come to understand that Giovanni had done his best with all that had been thrust upon him in what should have been his declining years.

Seven children.

Eight, if you included Nate, his son's illegitimate child.

'I've had many visitors this past couple of weeks,' Giovanni said.

'That's good.' Matteo sat down and Abby took a seat to his right and Matteo held her hand.

Matteo really was nervous, Abby realised as he addressed his grandfather. 'We've got some good news for you.'

They didn't drag it out. Abby handed over the magnificent box and Giovanni let out a small cry of recognition.

'This is the box…' Even that thrilled Giovanni.

It was walnut and gleaming and his fingers struggled with the small clasp and Matteo watched as Abby helped him to open it and the necklace was finally revealed to him.

'Oh...'

Had Abby doubted—and she *had* doubted whether or not she should give up her mother's necklace—those last niggles left her then.

Giovanni's blue eyes filled with tears and his old hands took out the necklace and he gazed upon stones that would never diminish with age.

'You cannot know what this means to me to hold it again.'

'We don't need to know,' Abby said. 'An old man must have his secrets after all.'

'Matteo told you the tale?'

'He did.'

'Matteo told me that he couldn't remember.'

'I know I did,' Matteo said. 'Of course I remember.'

Giovanni looked from the necklace to his grandson, who he had struggled so hard to love.

'I was wrong,' Giovanni said. 'To compare you to your father...'

'Can we leave it?' Matteo said, as was his preferred method.

'We've left too many things unsaid,' Giovanni responded and then he looked down to the necklace as if it gave him strength to speak from the heart.

'To see the damage my son did was more than I could take. When I took in his children I wanted to put things right but I was lost in my own regret and grief.'

'I know.'

'You look like him,' Giovanni said. 'You laugh and you act like him and I was scared for you.'

'I know that you were,' Matteo said. 'But you don't need to be now. I've got a new addiction.'

'Motor racing.'

'Two actually,' Matteo said but Giovanni was looking at the necklace and back in his own world again.

'If I could have a day with it,' Giovanni said and he looked to Abby. 'Just some time to remember...'

'It's yours,' Abby interrupted.

'No.' Giovanni shook his head. 'It was your mother's. Matteo told me he would never take it from you, that you had based your racing team around these stones.'

'My mother had green eyes,' Abby said. 'I remember them. I don't need this necklace to do that. It's yours. It's back where it belongs.'

She looked to Matteo because Giovanni was crying and really was distressed and maybe now wasn't the time to tell him the rest of the news that they had to share.

'Abby should have it to give it to her children...' Giovanni insisted.

'Maybe she shall,' Matteo responded. 'Given that it's staying in the family.'

Giovanni frowned.

'We're not just here to give you the necklace,' Matteo said.

'You two...' Giovanni had been accused one too

many times of jumping in and he was struggling not to now. 'You are engaged.' His eyes lit up again as Abby held out her hand for Giovanni to admire the ring. 'When did this happen?'

'Two weeks ago,' Matteo said. 'We're getting married in, oh, about ten minutes from now.'

'I don't understand.'

'You don't have to,' Matteo said. 'Alma has everything ready, the celebrant is here…'

'Your brothers and sisters…' Giovanni went to rise, to share the news with family, but Matteo shook his head.

'We want it to be very small,' Matteo explained. 'Abby has been through a lot and we don't want to make a big fuss. The press will no doubt find out but it will be long over and done with by the time that they do. We're marrying now, by the lake with you and Alma as our witnesses…'

The drapes had been drawn and now Matteo pulled them back on a delicious setting sun.

Beneath the tree he had once fallen from was an arch of white roses and soon they would stand there and make their vows.

Alma had already changed and had a suit waiting for Giovanni.

Abby's hair had already been done and she changed into a very simple, coffee-coloured chiffon dress and the same jewelled sandals that had seen her through favourite days.

It was as simple and as beautiful as that.

Abby topped up her lipstick and the least nervous bride walked slowly with Matteo and his grandfather outside and then Giovanni took a seat with Alma.

It was the smallest, most intimate of weddings.

Abby didn't wear the necklace; today it was *their* memories they made. Instead Giovanni held one of his Lost Mistresses in his hands as he sat and watched his wayward grandson stand before the woman he loved and offer his vows.

'I will always take care of you,' Matteo said. 'I know that I shall. You have made love possible for me and I will never forget that. I love you.'

Abby's words were similar. 'I will always be there for you as you are for me. You have made love possible for me and I will never forget that. I love you too.'

She looked into his dark eyes and she had never known such pure happiness, acceptance and absolute trust.

He slipped on a ring—a very simple band was all that was needed to set off such a magnificent engagement ring—and then Abby slipped a somewhat heavier band on his finger.

Matteo examined it.

It was a simple platinum band but there was just the tiniest emerald set into the metal.

'That's a bit blingy.' Matteo smiled, because not only hadn't he seen it, he'd never, not once, envisaged wearing a ring.

Proceedings paused for a moment but no one seemed to mind.

'Wear the stone facing down, then,' Abby said and Matteo did so.

It was never coming off!

And now, the celebrant told them, they were husband and wife.

'We should call the family…' Giovanni said to Alma as the bride and groom kissed. He wanted dinner, celebrations, but though Matteo loved his grandfather tonight was theirs.

'We're going to go,' Matteo said, holding Abby's hand. 'We just wanted to share the special day with you.'

He gave Alma a kiss and thanked her for helping in the arrangements and then he embraced his frail grandfather.

'What had happened to the other Lost Mistresses?' Abby asked as she said her goodbyes.

'Another time,' Matteo hastily broke in. They'd be here for hours if Giovanni started and Matteo had other plans for tonight! 'We've got our honeymoon to get to.'

They left his grandfather smiling, holding on to the necklace and sitting looking out across the lake and, yes, they had a honeymoon to get to, but Matteo went back for one more goodbye.

'I love you.'

He did.

It didn't roll off his tongue easily as it did when he said it to Abby, but Matteo meant it.

'I love you,' Giovanni said.

That was all.

They had come full circle and there were no more sorrys to be had.

Matteo drove them to the airport and in his complicated, somehow seamless world, there a driver was waiting to return the car to his home.

Their home.

Abby's head was still spinning; she hadn't come back to earth since the day that they had met and she somehow doubted she ever would.

At least not to the same one he had swept her away from.

'Where are we going?' Abby asked as they took their seats and, because it was a private jet, in a matter of moments they were heading off. As they hit cruise level the flight attendants moved into the sleeping area and then the captain's voice came on.

'Congratulations, Mr and Mrs Di Sione, on your marriage. With a tailwind our flight will take approximately seven hours.'

Matteo took her hand and led her to the sleeping area and the crew had done them proud.

There were petals strewn on the bed and there was a feast of champagne and so many delicacies that for a moment she took her eye off the groom.

There were cupcakes that looked like miniature wedding cakes but when Abby bit into one it was filled with a rich chocolate mousse.

'Seven hours' flying time,' Matteo said and he took her in his arms. 'Whatever will we do?'

'Is this a mystery flight?'

'No.' Matteo shook his head. 'We're going to Paris, the city of romance. I think it's time to make up for some lost time—neither of us have ever really dated. I'm going to put that right.'

He put her whole world to rights and Abby did the same for him.

'So no mystery,' Matteo said. 'It's just the start of our adventure.'

* * * * *

*If you enjoyed this book, look out for
the next instalment of*
THE BILLIONAIRE'S LEGACY:
*THE DI SIONE SECRET BABY
by Maya Blake
Coming next month*

Turn the page for an exclusive extract of
SLEEPLESS IN MANHATTAN
the first book in USA TODAY *bestselling author*
Sarah Morgan's enthralling new trilogy,
FROM MANHATTAN WITH LOVE*!*

PAIGE STOOD FOR a moment, thinking how unpredictable life was.

Who would have thought that herself, Eva and Frankie losing their jobs would have turned out so well?

Urban Genie existed only because life had laid a twist in her path.

Change had been forced on her, but it had proved to be a good thing.

Instead of fighting it, she should embrace it.

What had Jake said?

Sometimes you have to let life happen.

Maybe she should try to do that a bit more.

And maybe one day she'd look back and realize that *not* being with Jake was the best thing that could have happened—because if she'd been with Jake she wouldn't have met—

Who?

Would she ever meet someone who made her feel the way Jake did?

She stood leaning on the railing, gazing at the city she loved.

The lights of Manhattan sparkled like a thousand stars against a midnight sky and now, finally, as the last of the guests made their way to the elevators, she allowed herself a moment to enjoy it.

"Time to relax and celebrate, I think."

Jake's voice came from behind her and she turned to find him holding two glasses of champagne. He handed her one. "To Urban Genie."

"I don't drink while I'm working." And while Jake was present this was definitely still work.

She knew better than to lower her guard a second time.

"The guests have gone. You're no longer working. Your job is done."

"I'm not off duty until the clear-up has finished." And then tomorrow would be the follow-up, the post-mortem. Discussions on what they might have done differently. They'd unpick every part of the event and put it back together again. By the time they'd finished they'd have found every weak spot and strengthened it.

"I don't think one glass of champagne is going to impair your ability to supervise that. Congratulations." He tapped his glass against hers. "Spectacular. Any new business leads?"

"Plenty. First up is a baby shower next week. Not much time to prepare, but it's a good event."

He winced. "A baby shower is *good*?"

"Yes. Partly because the woman throwing it for her pregnant colleague is CEO of a fashion importer. But all business is good."

"Chase Adams is impressed. By tomorrow word will have got around that Urban Genie is the best event concierge company in Manhattan. Prepare to be busy."

"I'm prepared."

His praise warmed her. Her heart lifted.

He stood next to her and the brush of his sleeve against her bare arm made her shiver.

His gaze collided briefly with hers and she thought she saw a blaze of heat, but then he looked away and she did, too, her face burning.

She was doing it again. Imagining things.

And it had to stop.

It had to stop right now.

No more embarrassing herself. No more embarrassing *him*.

She turned her head to look at him but he was staring straight ahead, his handsome face blank of expression.

"Thank you," she said.

"For what?"

"For asking us to do this. For giving us free rein and no budget. For trusting us. For inviting influential people and decision-makers. For making Urban

Genie happen." She realized how much she owed him. "I hate accepting help—"

"I know, but that isn't what happened here. You did it yourself, Paige."

"But I wouldn't have been able to do it without you. I'm grateful. If you hadn't suggested it, pushed me that night on the terrace, I wouldn't have done it." She breathed in. Now was as good a time as any to say everything that needed to be said. And if she said it aloud maybe it would help both of them. "There's something else—" She saw him tense and felt a flash of guilt that he felt the need to be defensive around her. *Definitely* time to clear the air. "I owe you an apology."

"For what?"

"For misreading the situation the other night. For making things awkward between us. I was..." She hesitated, trying to find the right words. "I guess you could say I was doing an Eva. I was looking for things that weren't there. I was close to panic and you were trying to distract me. I understand that now. I don't want you feeling that you have to avoid me, or be careful around me. I'd never want that. I—"

"Don't. Don't apologize."

He gripped the railing and she noticed his knuckles were white.

"I wanted to clear it up, that's all. It was a kiss. Didn't mean anything. Two people trapped in an elevator, one of whom was feeling vulnerable." *Shut up right now, Paige.* "I know I'm not your type. I know you don't have those feelings. I'm like your little sister. I get that. So—"

"Oh, for— *Seriously?*" He interrupted her with a low growl and finally turned to face her. "After what happened the other night you really think I see you as *a little sister*? You think I could kiss you that way if I felt like that about you?"

She stared at him, her heart drumming a rhythm against her chest. "I thought— You said— I thought you saw me that way."

"Yeah, well, I tried." He gave a humorless laugh and drained his champagne in one mouthful. "God knows, I tried. I've done everything short of asking Matt for a baby photo of you and sticking that to my wall. Nothing works. And do you know why? Because I *do* have feelings, you're *not* little and you're not my damn *sister.*"

Shock struck her like a bolt of lightning.

They were the only two people left on the terrace. Just them and the Manhattan night. The buildings rose around them—dark shapes enveloping them in intimate shadows and the shimmer of light.

The storm clouds were gathering, creating ominous shadows in the dark sky.

The sudden lick of wind held the promise of rain.

Paige was oblivious. The sky might have come crashing down and she wouldn't have noticed.

Her mouth was so dry she could hardly form the

words. "But if you feel that way, if you do have feelings, why do you keep saying—" She stumbled over the words, confused. "Why haven't you ever done anything about it?"

"Why do you think?"

There was a cynical, bitter edge to Jake's tone that didn't fit the nature of their conversation. None of the pieces fitted. She couldn't think. Everything about her had ceased to function.

"Because of Matt?"

"Partly. He'd kick my butt. And I wouldn't blame him." He stared down at his hands, as if they were something that didn't belong to him. As if he was worried about what they might do.

"Because you're not interested in relationships—or 'complications' as you call them?"

"Exactly."

"But sex doesn't have to be a relationship. It can just be sex. You said so yourself."

"Not with you."

His tone was harsh and she took a step back, shocked. They'd often argued, baited each other, but she'd never heard that edge of steel in his voice before.

"Why? What's different about me?"

"I'm not going to screw you and walk away, Paige. That's not going to happen."

"Because of our friendship? Because you're worried it would be awkward?"

"Yeah, that, too."

"Too? What else?" She stared at him, bemused.

He was silent.

"Jake? What else?"

He swore under his breath. "Because I care about you. I don't want to hurt you. There's already been enough damage to your heart. You don't need more."

The first raindrops started to fall.

Paige was still oblivious.

Her head spun with questions. *Where? What? Why? How much?* "So you— Wait—" She struggled to make sense of it. "You're saying that you've been *protecting* me? No. That can't be true. You're the only one who *doesn't* protect me. When everyone else is wrapping me in cotton wool, you handle me as though you're throwing the first pitch at a game."

He didn't protect her. He *didn't*. Not Jake.

She waited for him to agree with her, to confirm that he didn't protect her.

He was silent.

There was a throbbing in her head. She lifted her fingers to her forehead and rubbed. The storm was closing in—she could feel it. And not just in the sky above her.

"I *know* you don't protect me." She tried to focus, tried to examine the information and shook her head. "Just the other night, when we found out we'd lost our jobs, Matt was sympathetic but you were brutal. I was ready to cry, but you made me so *angry* and—"

She stared at him, understanding. She felt the color drain from her face. "You did it on purpose. You made me angry on purpose."

"You get more done when you're angry," he said flatly. "And you needed to get things done."

No denial.

He'd goaded her. Galvanized her into action.

"You challenge every idea I have." She felt dizzy. "We fight. All the time. If I say something is black, you say it's white."

He stood in silence, not bothering to deny it, and she shook her head in disbelief.

"You *make* me angry. You do that on purpose. Because if I'm angry with you, then I'm not—" She'd been blind. She breathed hard, adjusting to this new picture of their relationship. The first boom of thunder split the air but she ignored it. "How long? How long, Jake?"

"How long, what?" He yanked at his bow tie with impatient fingers.

His gaze shifted from hers. He looked like a man who wanted to be anywhere but with her.

"How long have you cared? How long have you been p-protecting me?" She stumbled over the word—and the thought.

He ran his hand over his jaw. "Since I walked through the door of that damn hospital room and saw you sitting on the bed in your Snoopy T-shirt, with that enormous smile on your face. You were so brave. The most frightened brave person I'd ever seen. And you tried so hard not to let anyone see it. I have *always* protected you, Paige. Except for the other night, when I let my guard down."

But he'd been protecting her then, too. He'd been taking care of her when she'd been so terrified she hadn't known what to do.

"So you thought I was brave, but not strong? Not strong enough to cope alone without protection? I don't understand. I thought you weren't interested, that you didn't want this, and now I discover—" It was a struggle to process it. "So this whole time you *did* care about me. You *do*."

Rain was falling steadily now, landing in droplets on his jacket and her hair.

"Paige—"

"The kiss the other night—"

"Was a mistake."

"But it was real. It wasn't because I was a pair of red lips in an elevator. All these days, months, *years* I've been telling myself you didn't feel anything. All the time I've been confused because my instincts were so wrong and I couldn't understand why. But now I do. They weren't wrong. *I* wasn't wrong."

"Maybe you weren't."

"So why let me think that?"

"Because it was easier."

"Easier than what? Telling me the truth? News flash—and, by the way, I thought you knew this—

I don't want to be protected. I want to live my life. You're the one who's always telling me to take more risks."

"Yeah, well, that proves you shouldn't listen to anything I tell you. We should go inside before you catch pneumonia."

He eased away from the railings and she caught his arm.

"I'll go inside when I decide to go inside." The rain was soaking her skin. "What happens now?"

"Nothing. I know you don't want to be protected but that's tough, Paige, because that's what I'm doing. I'm not what you're looking for and I never have been. We don't want the same thing. There's a car waiting downstairs to take you and the other two home. Make sure you use it."

Without giving her a chance to respond, Jake strode away from her toward the bank of elevators and left her standing there, alone in the glittering cityscape, watching the entire shape of her life change. Another twist. Another turn. The unexpected.

*Don't miss SLEEPLESS IN MANHATTAN
by Sarah Morgan, available from HQN Books.*

COMING NEXT MONTH FROM

Presents

Available July 19, 2016

#3449 THE DI SIONE SECRET BABY
The Billionaire's Legacy
by Maya Blake

Charity CEO Allegra Di Sione can't fail in her mission to retrieve her grandfather's beloved Fabergé box from Sheikh Rahim Al-Hadi, which is why she gets caught in Rahim's sumptuous bedroom trying to steal it!

#3450 CARIDES'S FORGOTTEN WIFE
by Maisey Yates

After a car accident erases his memories, Leon Carides remembers nothing, except Rose's sparkling blue eyes. Now he'll do anything to claim the wife he'd left behind...including taking her to his bed!

#3451 THE PLAYBOY'S RUTHLESS PURSUIT
Rich, Ruthless and Renowned
by Miranda Lee

Playboy tycoon Jeremy Barker-Whittle isn't short on stunning women, but Alice Waterhouse is a challenge he can't refuse. But when he discovers Alice's carefully guarded innocence, he must forget this delicate beauty...until Alice shocks him by offering her virginity!

#3452 CROWNED FOR THE PRINCE'S HEIR
One Night With Consequences
by Sharon Kendrick

Dress designer Lisa Bailey broke off her fling with Luc, knowing her affair with the royal could never go anywhere. But after a one-off date "for old times' sake," there are consequences that tie her to Luc forever...

#3453 MARRYING HER ROYAL ENEMY
Kingdoms & Crowns
by Jennifer Hayward
Most women would kill to be draped in ivory and walking up the aisle toward King Kostas Laskos. But Stella Constantinides naively bared her heart to Kostas to disastrous effect once before and this feisty princess refuses to be his pawn ever again.

#3454 HIS MISTRESS FOR A WEEK
by Melanie Milburne
Years ago, Clementine Scott clashed spectacularly with arrogant architect Alistair Hawthorne and swore she'd never have anything to do with him again! But when Clem's brother disappears with Alistair's stepsister, she's forced to go with Alastair to Monte Carlo to retrieve them!

#3455 IN THE SHEIKH'S SERVICE
by Susan Stephens
Sheikh Shazim Al Q'Aqabi must resist his instant attraction to mysterious dancer Isla Sinclair, for duty is Shazim's only mistress. Until Isla is revealed as the prize winner who will travel to the desert to work with him...making their chemistry impossible to ignore.

#3456 CLAIMING HIS WEDDING NIGHT
by Louise Fuller
Addie Farrell's marriage to casino magnate Malachi King lasted exactly one day, until she discovered their love was a sham. Now Addie must prepare to face her husband—and their dangerously seductive chemistry—once again!

YOU CAN FIND MORE INFORMATION ON UPCOMING HARLEQUIN® TITLES, FREE EXCERPTS AND MORE AT WWW.HARLEQUIN.COM.

HPCNM0716RB

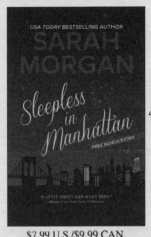

$7.99 U.S./$9.99 CAN.

EXCLUSIVE
Limited Time Offer

$1.⁰⁰ OFF

USA TODAY Bestselling Author
SARAH MORGAN

introduces From Manhattan with Love,
a sparkling new trilogy about three best friends
embracing life—and love—in New York.

Paige Walker loves a challenge, but can she
convince a man who trusts no one to take a
chance on forever?

Sleepless in
Manhattan

Available May 31, 2016.
Pick up your copy today!

HQN™

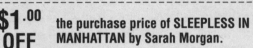

"I came here to set a few things straight with you," Rahim
sneered, deeply resentful that she'd led him to question
himself when there was no doubt where his destiny lay.
"You thought what happened in Dar-Aman wouldn't go
unchallenged. You were wrong."

Allegra's hand jerked to her stomach, her eyes more
vivid against her ashen colour. "No. Please…"

From across the room, Rahim saw her sway. With a
curse, he charged forward and caught her as her legs gave
way. It occurred to him then that she hadn't answered him
when he'd asked what ailed her. Swinging her up into his
arms, he carried her to the sofa and laid her down.

With a low moan, she tried to get up. Rahim stayed her
with a firm hand. "I'm going to get you some water. Then
you'll tell me what's wrong with you. And what the hell
you're doing giving long speeches and photo ops when
you should be in bed."

Her mouth pursed mutinously for a moment before she gave a small nod.

Rising, he crossed to the bar and poured a glass of water. She'd sat up by the time he returned. Silently she took the water and sipped, her wary eyes following him as he sat on the sturdy coffee table directly in front of her.

"Now tell me what's wrong with you."

The sleek knot at her nape had come undone during the journey to the sofa, and twin falls of chocolate-brown hair framed her face as she bent her head. Rahim gritted his teeth against the urge to brush it back, soothe whatever was troubling her, reassure her that he meant her no harm.

He was so busy fighting his baser urges, and sternly reminding himself that he was in the right and she in the wrong, that he didn't hear her whispered words.

"What did you say?"

Her jerky inhale wobbled the glass in her hands. "I said I'm not sick, but I can't go to prison because I'm pregnant." She raised her head then and stared back at him with eyes black with despair. "I'm carrying your child, Rahim."

Don't miss
THE DI SIONE SECRET BABY
by Maya Blake,
available August 2016 wherever
Harlequin Presents® books and ebooks are sold.

www.Harlequin.com